Sunset After The Storm

Michelle Sullivan

Sunset after the Storm

Published by: Michelle Sullivan 2017

www.authormichellesullivan.com

Facebook: Michelle Sullivan- Author

Instagram: michellesullivanauthor

Cover design by: John Connell

johnconnell.crevado.com

To Mom,

When I cried, you wiped my tears.

When I laughed, you laughed with me.

When I screamed and yelled... well, you usually sent me to my room.
But when I calmed down, I got the best hugs ever!

When I said I wanted to do something,

You told me I could do anything.

Thank you for always being my biggest fan!

You were always by my side... and even now, from Heaven, you are still guiding me.

I love you Mom and I miss you each and every day!

XOXO

Prologue

Scotti

It's funny how, when something big happens, you suddenly start running a slideshow of your entire life in your head. Everything from as far back as you can remember starts replaying over and over and you start thinking of things you wish you did or didn't do or things you wish you would have done better. That is what is happening in my head right now.

Two days ago, I had some medical testing done after ending up in the emergency room and today, I am sitting in the waiting room of my doctors' office, awaiting the results, but in my heart, I already know what they will be.

I look around this room and each person that is here has someone with them. There is hand holding, some hugging, arms around each other and an occasional peck on the lips. I look next to me and that chair is empty, it has always been empty and it will always be empty. The slideshow that is replaying in my head isn't very long. I have had a shit life since pretty much the day I was born and sitting in this office shows me that it won't be improving anytime soon.

"Miss Marks?" I look up to see a nurse standing there, trying to keep a neutral face but I can already read pity all over it. "The doctor is ready to see you now."

I slowly get up and follow the nurse down the hall into a well-furnished office. I take a seat on one of the chairs across from his desk and fold my hands in my lap. My heart is not racing, my hands are not shaking and my legs are not bouncing. Maybe there is something very wrong with me because I don't feel nervous in a way that I would think most people would when they are going to find out what I am going to find out.

I look around his office and see pictures with inspirational sayings on them. Stuff about staying positive and getting up when you fall and I find myself rolling my eyes as I am reading them. None of those quotes or even thinking those things is going to change my diagnosis today. Nothing I say or do is going to cure me. Now I am starting to feel angry and I find myself wanting to run out of this office before I even have to see my doctor.

"Good afternoon Scotti," Doctor Hammond says as he walks in his office and sits down behind his desk.

"Hi Doctor Hammond," I say quietly, wishing I would have thought of my escape plan just one minute sooner.

He opens up a file that he carried in with him, then folds his hands neatly on top of it and looks at me. He doesn't need to say anything. I already know. I see it in his face just like I saw it on that nurse's face a few minutes ago.

I take a deep breath and blow it out slowly then look him in the eyes. "You don't need to say it. Just tell me doc, where do we go from here?"

One

Mason

Now

To say that this story is your typical happily ever after would be a lie, so I won't even bother. To say that this is a story of the strongest love that two people can have, now that is the absolute truth. There are a couple times that I have been asked, if I knew then what I know now, would I have just walked away and never experienced the pain that I am experiencing in this very moment? My answer is always the same… never in a million fucking years! Walking away means never meeting Scotti, means never experiencing the love that I have with her, means never seeing that beautiful smile when I wake up each morning, means never seeing her look of pleasure each time we make love, means never feeling her touch and means never falling in love. Why in the hell would I ever walk away from that? My heart is breaking as I sit here, next to my wife's hospital bed, watching her suffering day in and day out, knowing that we don't have much more time together. There is nothing more that the doctors can do to help her, so now they are just keeping her as comfortable as possible. She sleeps a lot but there are still little moments of her being awake, when I can look into her beautiful blue eyes and remember her before she was sick, before she was pumped full of drugs. I hate to use the term "full of life" but truth be told, there is that too. She was so happy and carefree. She had been dealt a shitty life but she didn't let that stop her from experiencing happiness. As long as she was breathing and her heart was still beating she figured she could get through anything. Until she got really sick, I very rarely saw her without a smile on her face. Sure, she had her times of anger or sadness but they didn't last long. The day I met her was one of the hardest days that she ever had, yet she still managed to find some sort of happiness. I will never forget that day for as long as I live because as far as I am concerned, it was the day I met the most incredible person I will ever know. It was the day I met the person that was going to change my life forever.

Then

Work, run along the beach, work some more, sleep for a few hours, repeat. This moment, at the end of the day, as the sun is setting and there is a chill in the air, this is the time that I feel like the weight of the world is off my shoulders, when I can finally breathe and not think about my fucked up life. Running is my getaway, my peace if you will. I don't do it in order to stay in shape; I really don't care at all about that. I need to do this because too much quiet time allows my mind to go to places it has no business going anymore.

I just had my 30th birthday, a birthday that I spent alone because I have basically treated everyone in my life like complete shit. Who would even want to be around me? Sure, I now own a successful business and I treat my employees well but they are just that- employees. As soon as the day is over they go their way, and I go mine.

I have nobody but myself to blame for any of this. I decided to spend many years of my life as nothing but a low life drunk. Because of that addiction I lost my home, my family and what few friends I had. My parents were both killed in a car accident, ironically by a drunk driver, when I was 13 years old. I was raised by my Aunt and Uncle, who did not deserve the shit storm that I created when I walked into their perfect life. When I was 15 I started hanging out with a crowd of older kids, who were always able to get beer and pot. I never got in to smoking anything but the drinking, now that is something I never had a problem doing. By the time I was 16, I was pretty much drunk daily, skipping school and getting into fights. My Aunt really tried to do what she could to help me but my behavior was starting to put a strain on her marriage so on my eighteenth birthday, she kicked me out, and I have not seen nor spoken to her or my Uncle since that day.

Since I spent my entire high school career drunk I never graduated so I decided to sober up long enough to take my GED so I could at least get a job, mainly so I had money to buy more booze. I had a friend, and I use that term loosely, that was letting me crash on his couch so at least I had a roof over my head, although even in my drunk fog I knew that wouldn't last forever.

I passed the GED test with flying colors and as soon as I got my certificate, I applied for what felt like a million jobs. Finally, I got a call back to interview at the local market stocking shelves. It wasn't a dream career but it was something. I interviewed, got the job and started immediately. It was a good thing that I got the job when I did, because two weeks later my friend kicked my ass out, saying that I had stolen some vodka from his refrigerator. He was right, I did steal it, I was that out of control. I didn't even have a car to sleep in so I spent about a week sleeping in parks, under bridges, wherever I could find a place that wouldn't be visible to a passing cop.

One day, when I was clocking in at work, I saw a "roommate wanted" ad posted on the bulletin board. The person renting it was a cashier named Cara. She was annoying as fuck but I needed a place to live so I spoke to her about it, made all the necessary arrangements and within a couple of days I was moving in. Cara liked me, as more than just a friend but I wanted nothing to do with relationships, certainly not with Cara the crazy cashier. I don't think that I am a bad looking guy and I did get the occasional attention from women but at that time, all I cared about was getting my next drink. I will admit though, I was horny, so we ended up having sex with the understanding that it was just a fuck and nothing more.

That was my life for several years, working at the market by day, getting drunk and fucking Cara by night. It was all great until she decided to find a man that she was going to spend the rest of her life with. I was no longer wanted or needed but there was no way I could find my own place on the shitty salary I was making so I decided to find another job, and I did, as a fucking car salesman.

I hated this job. At least as a stocker at the market I had minimal contact with customers. As a salesperson, the only way I earned a paycheck was to talk to customers. I was doing pretty good there for a while, making a decent living and was even able to afford my own apartment. In between customers I would sneak a few drinks here and there to keep me going. Well, that came back to bite me in the ass one day.

A new, sweet looking ride came on the lot and I decided I was going to take it for a little spin, just around the block. Well, as soon as I drove off the lot I floored it… right into a telephone pole. The cops showed up, my boss showed up, my blood alcohol level was above the legal limit so I lost my job and was thrown in jail, all in one day.

That was when I finally decided to turn my life around. I served my time, got out and found a new job working in construction and most importantly, I got sober. After a few years, I decided I really liked the construction business and my boss really liked me so that's when I decided to take it over since he was ready to retire. It wasn't easy at first, in fact I didn't think the company would make it, but it slowly picked up and is now fairly successful. I upgraded from an apartment to a house and was even able to buy a truck. I am a workaholic but I guess it is better than where I was a few years ago.

I have been running for about two miles when I see a woman up ahead, sitting on the sand, knees up to her chest and her head buried in them. I start to move my way around her but as I am getting closer I notice that her body is shaking because she is crying.

I slow down to a walk and slowly approach her to make sure she is ok. I get to where I am standing right next to her and clear my throat to let her know that I am there. She slowly lifts her head and wipes her face with her hands but never looks over at me, instead stares out into the ocean. I kneel down so I am more at her level and although I am only looking at the side of her face, I can tell that she is beautiful. She has long blonde hair that is blowing in the breeze, smooth skin from her face, all the way to her toes that are partially buried in the sand, and she smells amazing. She takes a deep breath and slowly starts turning her head towards me and as soon as her blue eyes look into mine, I fall backwards on my ass, but I never take my eyes off her. I have never seen eyes that color. They are the bluest blue I have ever seen, bluer than the sky and so incredibly beautiful, even if they are puffy from crying. She smiles at me and it literally takes my breath away. I try to speak to her but nothing is coming out. I continue to stare at her as she continues smiling, or should I say smirking, at me. I don't know what just happened but I knew at that moment, that my life would never be the same.

Two

Mason

Now

"What are you smiling at?" Scotti asks me in a quiet voice.

I look up and she is staring at me with a weak smile. "I was just remembering the day we met." I told her, grabbing her hand and pulling it up to my lips.

"That certainly was a good day, well, sort of."

"It was a great day." I pick up her cup of water and hold the straw to her lips but she shakes her head. "Baby, you need to drink something, please."

She shakes her head again, "I'm not thirsty." She says, and then turns her head away from me.

I set the cup down then sit next to her on her bed, "Scotti, look at me please."

She slowly turns to look at me with tears slowly running down her face. I use my hand to wipe the tears then lean down to kiss her. "What can I do to dry those tears, baby?" I know there is nothing I can do, but I always ask anyway.

"Slap me so I will wake up from this nightmare." As soon as the last word is out of her mouth the tears begin to fall even faster.

"I want more than anything for this all to be a nightmare. I wish I could fix this." I feel the moisture building in my own eyes but the last thing I want to do is show my emotions to her when she is hurting so bad right now. I turn my head and start to get off the bed but Scotti grabs my arm.

"Honey, please don't hide your feelings from me. I have it easy. I am going to die and be done with all of this soon, but you are going to have to live in this world without me. You will be the one suffering. You definitely have the shit end of this stick."

That is one thing about Scotti and me. We don't hold anything back from each other. I don't walk around, pretending that I will be fine after she dies. I don't put a smile on my face and say how great it is that soon she will no longer be suffering. Nope, I don't say any of that because I already know I will not be fine, not one fucking bit. I will be a mess and I know it. Losing her was always what I have dreaded the most and now there is not a damn thing I can do to stop it. I honestly don't know how I am going to live my life without her in it but unfortunately, I have no choice. She is right; I do have the shit end of this stick.

"I'm sorry; I don't mean to turn away. I am just having a hard time coming to terms with this and I feel like a dick for showing that right in front of you when you are the one lying here sick."

Scotti reached up and rubbed my cheek, "You know you can tell me anything, no matter what. We promised each other we wouldn't hide anything from one another again."

"You're right," I took a deep breath then laid my head next to her and closed my eyes, "I am just so fucking pissed right now and I don't know how to handle this anger. Back in the day I would turn to the bottle but I promised you I would never do that again so I am just trying to figure out what to do."

Scotti squeezed my hand, well as much as her weak body could, "I am pissed too, now more than ever. Go back to the memories, Mason. When you thought I was sleeping I was watching you and you were smiling, and that is something I don't see you do much of lately. Inside those memories is where you need to be right now. Those memories are going to keep you going." She turned her head and started to close her eyes. "I need to take a little nap anyway. I'm exhausted."

I pulled her blanket up to cover her then sat next to her and rubbed the top of her head until her eyes were closed and she fell asleep. I gently kissed her then stood up and decided to take a walk and get some fresh air. When I got outside I went to a place that I have been several times, a grassy area with trees, benches and very few people. I walked over and sat down on the grass and rested my head against the tree. I closed my eyes and my thoughts went back to that day on the beach. The day that I met Scotti, the day when I knew I found someone special, and the day when I almost let it all go…

Then

"What is your name?" I asked her quietly, hoping she would stay and talk to me and not run away.

"Scottlyn, but I go my Scotti." Fuck, not only was she a beautiful woman but she had a beautiful name to go along with it. "What is your name?" She asked me.

"Mason. Not quite as nice as your name." I said, getting another one of those beautiful smiles out of her.

"I like it," she said, then turned her head back to the ocean.

We stayed quiet for a few minutes but I was still bothered by her crying earlier. "Scotti, is everything ok with you?"

She looked over at me and smiled, "Of course, why do you ask?"

"Well, when I first walked up to you it looked like you were crying."

She nodded her head, "I was, but I am feeling better now."

"Would you like to talk about it?" I asked her. I have never been much of a talker or listener for that matter, but for some reason I want to hear everything that she has to say and I didn't want to leave her.

She took a deep breath, "Well, where should I start? I got fired today, from a job I hated but at least it was a job. I have no home so I was hoping that I would be able to save up enough soon to get a place to live but instead I will continue staying at the women's shelter. Oh, and to top it all off, I have to start chemo soon so I will be sick, bald and unemployed."

Holy shit! "You have cancer?" She nodded and I felt like my heart stopped. I know she told me a lot more than that but the second I heard the word 'chemo', I couldn't remember anything else she said. I literally felt my heart stop in that very moment. I just met this woman, felt drawn to her for reasons that make no fucking sense to me at all and now she just told me that she has cancer. I don't even know what to say so I reach over, grab her hand and squeeze it.

She smiles at me but doesn't pull it away, "Bet you wish you would have never asked, huh?" She said with a smile. How the hell is this woman smiling after the day that she had?

I didn't know what to say so I just shook my head and turned away. "Oh no you don't," she said, "don't shut down on me now just because I told you all of that. You asked, so I answered. If you can't handle it, you are more than welcome to leave."

Just the thought of leaving her gave me a stomach ache, "I'm sorry, I wasn't expecting to hear all of that. I just needed a minute to process but I am good now." She smiled at me and nodded her head. "If you don't mind my asking, what kind of cancer did you have?"

"You may ask me anything. It's ovarian cancer. I had a hysterectomy about five weeks ago so if you are planning on me being your baby mama in the future you better run now before you fall in love with me and want to have a family." She was laughing but I wasn't. She took a deep breath then continued, "anyway, my doctor called me today and wants me to start chemotherapy so I can hardly wait for that next step." Although she was crying when I first saw her, she seems to be brushing all of this off like it is no big deal. She is making jokes about a disease that kills millions every year. I was starting to feel angry but I couldn't figure out why. Maybe I shouldn't let it bother me but it does. I quickly stood up and walked a few steps away from her.

"Well, it was nice meeting you, Mason." I turned around and Scotti was standing up and brushing sand off her ass. She reached down and picked up her shoes then turned to walk away but I jumped towards her and grabbed her arm, causing her to abruptly turn to me. "Mason, what the hell are you doing?"

I stood there and stared at her, not knowing what to say and not wanting her to walk away. "I don't want you to leave." I told her, being completely truthful.

She reached up with her free hand, gently placed it on my cheek and smiled, "I appreciate that, but I don't want to drag you into this mess. You seem like a really nice guy and it was very nice of you to stop and make sure I was okay but I am sure you have a nice life and I refuse to mess that up."

"Actually, I have a horrible life," I said, "and running on the beach is the only thing that clears my head. I normally don't run at this beach but I was drawn this way today, and now I know the reason."

"And what is that reason?" She asked me, looking me straight in the eyes.

"It was so I would meet you. Do you believe in that?"

She raised her eyebrows, "Do I believe in destiny? Sure, why not? But this is a bad time for that to happen." I started to say something but she raised her hand up to let her finish. "A few months ago I would have been ecstatic to meet you because I really like you and I felt comfortable with you right away, and I never feel comfortable with anyone. A few months ago I would have looked at you and had dirty thoughts about you because you are ridiculously hot. A few months ago I would have been silently hoping you would ask me out on a date and maybe even kiss me. A few months ago I wasn't sick, at least I didn't know I was, but today is different. Today I have chemo to get ready for. I will be very sick and losing my hair. This disease just ruined any chance I will ever have with you. As nice as you are and as much as I would love to get to know you better, I couldn't put you through that. I'm sorry."

She started to walk away then she stopped and walked back over to me. She lifted up on her toes, gently put her lips to my cheek and kissed me. "Thank you, Mason. I literally have nobody in my life and for just a short time, sitting here with you, I actually felt like I wasn't alone. I will never forget you for as long as I live." She smiled at me, then turned and walked away.

I called her name but she kept walking away from me. I fell to my knees and just watched her go, until I could no longer see her. What the hell did I just do? What kind of a piece of shit am I? How could I just let her walk away? She just told me she had nobody and now she is going to be going through treatments alone. There is no way I am going to let that happen. I jumped up and ran in the direction of where she disappeared but couldn't find her anywhere. Son of a bitch! I need to figure out where she is staying and where she will be having her chemo treatments because I will be damned if that was the last I have seen of that woman.

Three

Scotti

This is just my luck. I think I just met the most amazing and sexiest man to walk this Earth. He is at least six feet tall, he has short hair but not too short and gorgeous brown eyes that I could stare into for days. It figures I would meet him now, just weeks after I had all my female parts ripped from my body because of this piece of shit disease that I have, and days before I have a poison injected into my body that is going to make me the sickest I have ever been. To say that I am angry about this is an understatement. I may have a crappy life, but I always thought that maybe, one day, my luck would change and I would meet a great man, maybe have a couple of babies and a house, and be happy. After what happened to me by the hands of my last boyfriend, people would probably think I would never want to even talk to another man, let alone have another man touch me, but that is not at all how I think. My feeling is that Charlie, my asshole ex, was a lesson or maybe just a setback. Maybe I needed to go through hell with him so I would learn to appreciate what I had, when I finally had it. Now I meet

Mason, on the same day I not only lose my job, but my doctor tells me something that I have been dreading since I found out about this cancer. To be honest, I knew before today that something wasn't right, I just didn't know how bad it was until a few hours ago. I was hoping that I would find out the other tests were wrong, but instead I found out they were worse than what I thought. So here I am, walking away from this man that, for just a very short period of time, made me feel like I wasn't completely alone in this world. There is no way I can tell him what is really going on and there is no way I would ever want to drag him into this mess that is my life. Who knows what could have happened between us if it wasn't for this disease. For now, I will use that fairy tale to get me through the hell that I will soon be facing.

As I round the corner of my neighborhood I see several cop cars sitting in front of the women's shelter that I am currently living in. It doesn't even surprise me anymore. It means another pissed off man has found his wife or girlfriend there and is threatening her. This happens from time to time but luckily I don't have to worry about that.

Deciding that I don't want to be around that drama, I turn towards the park to be alone until the cops leave. I would go back to the beach, my absolute favorite place in the world, but I don't want to take the chance of running in to Mason again. I sit on the swing and imagine Mason's arms around me, kissing me and telling me he loves me. It's crazy to even think this about someone I just met but something about Mason made me happy. He seemed genuinely nice but the feelings in my heart and my stomach when I was talking to him, and now in my daydream, should not be happening, not to someone like me. He deserves a woman that can give him a future, not a woman who is sick. He deserves someone to grow old with and have babies with. He deserves someone so much better than me. Obviously, I will never be able to carry a child of my own but there are millions of children in the world that need good homes and I still had that dream for myself. One single doctors' appointment changed all of that though. One single doctors' appointment made my beautiful dream turn into an ugly nightmare.

I am getting to the point that I am starting to feel sorry for myself so that is my cue to get back home. It has hopefully been long enough for the craziness to die down. As I am walking back, my thoughts go to Mason again. He was so thoughtful and kind to me. The only person that is ever somewhat friendly to me is my oncologist. Not even my roommates like me much, but Mason seemed like he actually cared that I was upset and held my hand to comfort me. Fuck, why couldn't I have met this man before I was sick, while I still had hope that everything was going to be alright.

Four

Mason

It's been ten days since I last saw Scotti. After what felt like endless searching, I finally found the shelter that she is staying in. I haven't been to work since the day I met her which is the first time ever since I took over the company. My employees have been in constant contact with me, worrying that something is very wrong. I just tell them I have some family issues to deal with and since none of them know I don't even have a family, they have not questioned it.

Now I am standing outside this small house that is used as a women's shelter, waiting for Scotti to get here. According to the girl inside, she has been out all day. Since I know she doesn't have a job, I am sitting here, worried sick, wondering where she is. I get up to pace the sidewalk for about the fiftieth time when I see her walking towards the house.

"Where the hell have you been?" I ask her as I am quickly walking towards her.

She stops and looks a bit startled then anger takes over. "Excuse me? Don't talk to me like that! My whereabouts are none of your damn business!" She yells then walks around me towards the house, while mumbling something about me being a cranky asshole.

"Fuck, Scotti, I'm sorry," I say to her but she ignores my apology and keeps walking, "Scotti, please stop!"

She stops then turns around and walks toward me until she is toe to toe with me then slams her finger into my chest, "I talked to you briefly on the beach, that is it. You are not my boyfriend. Shit, you're not even my friend, so don't think you can come to my home and question me on anything, Mason!"

She turns away from me again and I can't help but smile at the fact that she remembers my name. I run past her and jump in front of her to get her to stop and grab both of her hands. "I'm so sorry. I just got worried about you. I shouldn't have yelled at you like that. Please don't be upset with me."

She stares at me, or should I say glares at me, but doesn't pull her hands away so I am hoping she is calming down. "You are a dick Mason!" She says, never looking away from me.

This woman is not only sexy but she is tough and I would love nothing more than to grab her face and pull her lips to mine, but since she just said we aren't even friends, I would probably be met with a fist in my face if I tried it. "You're right, I am a huge dick," I tell her.

"You will never talk to me like that again, right?" She says, pulling her hands away from mine and putting them on her hips.

"I will never talk to you like that again. I promise."

It took her a minute but finally she smiled at me. "Good. Now, how did you find me?"

I let out a breath that I didn't realize I was holding. She went from yelling and ready to rip my balls off to sweet and soft spoken and it was a huge turn on. I wanted to kiss her so bad, but instead I smiled at her, "It wasn't easy but I basically found every single women's shelter and just started going door to door. I never realized how many there were around here. When I got to this one they also told me they had never heard of you. But, I spotted something on the desk that had your name on it so I knew they were just telling me that for privacy reasons. After a lot of convincing and maybe a little sweet talking, the girl at the desk finally confirmed you lived here but you weren't home. Now here we are." I smiled at her but she looked angry.

"Fuck!" She yelled then started walking towards the house.

"Scotti, wait up! What's wrong?" I yelled to her as I was chasing after her.

She abruptly stopped, causing me to run in to her then turned around, "Mason, they aren't allowed to tell people who lives here just because someone sweet talks them. They can't do that! Most of the women that are staying at this shelter are hiding out from someone that abused them or are looking to hurt them. How do they know that you aren't one of those men?"

Holy shit, I didn't even think of that, I was just trying to find her but she is right. It was a lot easier to convince that girl that I was a friend then it should have been, but that is not what bothered me most, "Is someone trying to hurt you, Scotti?" I asked, and then held my breath, waiting for her answer.

She stared at me for a minute before answering quietly, "Not anymore."

I didn't know what she meant by that but I couldn't help but feel relief when she said it.

She turned back towards the house again but before she could walk two steps I gently grabbed her arm, "This is my fault Scotti. I should have never said anything to that girl. Please, let me take you to dinner and let's talk before you run in there and strangle her."

She nods her head then takes a deep breath, "Fine, I will go to dinner with you but she needs to be reported."

"You're right. Call whoever you need to from the car to report her. Then you won't have to be here when the shit hits the fan." She nods her head then we walk hand in hand over to my truck and I open the door for her. Once she is in and I close it, I sprint around to the drivers' side and jump in. "So, what are you hungry for?"

"Any place that serves chips and salsa," she said smiling.

"Mexican food it is." I started up the truck and took off. And that was the start of the best date of my life…

Scotti was so easy to talk to and I have never had so much fun in my entire life as I did that night at dinner. On our way to the restaurant, she used my phone and called the proper person to get that girl at the shelter reported. She was angry but she wasn't worried about herself, she was only worried about those other women at the shelter.

Once we got to the restaurant and sat down we started talking. I told her about my entire childhood from losing my parents to being drunk every day and she never batted an eye. She never judged me for the things I did wrong. She just smiled and told me how proud she was of me for turning my life around. This woman was a true angel.

"So, you have heard all about my life, now tell me about yours."

She smiled at me then took a deep breath, "Okay. Well, I don't know my parents. They are drug addicts that got busted when I was a baby. I went from foster home to foster home my entire childhood until I turned 18 and was aged out of the system. I was basically homeless for a couple of years until I met a man, who I thought was great at first and who promised to take care of me. I lived with him up until almost two years ago."

"What happened?" I asked her, feeling a jealousy inside.

"He died," She said as she grabbed a chip and popped in her mouth.

"I'm so sorry." I told her, now feeling terrible for getting jealous.

"Don't be, he was a piece of shit."

"How did he die?"

She shrugged her shoulders, "Got shot right in the chest. He died instantly."

I gasped, "Holy shit! Were you there when it happened?"

She slowly nodded her head and looked down, "Yes…"

"You are lucky that you didn't get hurt or killed too." I can't imagine what she must have gone through seeing someone get killed in cold blood.

She shrugged her shoulders, "That wasn't possible."

"What do you mean?" I asked her, confused.

She took a deep breath then looked me in the eyes, "Because, Mason, I'm the one that shot him."

Five

Mason

What. The. Fuck? Did I just hear that right?

"Yep, you heard it right." Scotti said, making me realize I had just said that out loud.

"I'm sorry, I guess I wasn't expecting you to say that."

"I would hope you weren't expecting that," she said smiling. Again, smiling, after just telling me she killed a man. What is the deal with this woman? "Look, you are freaking out so let me just tell you, I am not some murderer or anything. It was self-defense. It was either shoot him or die, so I shot him."

I felt like I needed time to process this information so I wasn't saying anything, I didn't know what to say. I heard Scotti's chair push against the floor and when I looked up she was standing. "What are you doing?" I asked her.

"Leaving. This was obviously way more than you bargained for and I don't blame you."

She reached for her purse and I grabbed her hand. "Please don't leave again."

"Mason, since I met you I have done nothing but lay out all this shit on you and I can tell this is too much for you to process. I don't want to keep doing this to you. I appreciate you talking to me and taking me to dinner but this is exactly why I don't have anyone in my life. I have way too much baggage."

"We both have baggage Scotti. Please, I would like to finish dinner and talk to you some more. I'm sorry I didn't have the perfect reaction to everything you have told me but all the information you have given me doesn't make me feel a bit different about you." And that was the God's honest truth. She could have told me she killed ten men and I would still want her sitting across from me.

She stood there for a minute, looking like she was contemplating everything I just said to her then finally she slowly sat back in her chair, and continued eating. I picked up my fork and starting eating too. For a few minutes, it was completely silent until... "He hurt me Mason," she said, almost whispering.

I looked up at her and she had set her fork down, had her hands folded in her lap and was looking at me with sadness in her eyes. "What did he do?" I asked her, although I wasn't really sure if I wanted to know.

She didn't immediately start talking. She took a deep breath and slowly let it out. "What didn't he do? He was charming when I met him and made me believe he actually cared about me. He continued with that act until the day I moved in with him and that is when the nightmare began. He would punch me, kick me, push me down the stairs, and pull my hair, anything to just be flat out mean. One evening, after listening to him berate me for hours, he actually had the nerve to ask me to have sex with him. I told him to go to hell and…" she stopped talking long enough to take a drink of water, "that was the first time that I was beaten unconscious, but it wouldn't be the last time."

I gasped loudly, shocked by what she was telling me and I didn't want to hear anymore, but she continued, "During our relationship I had both my legs broken, my right arm broken twice, several teeth knocked out and I can't even tell you the amount of stitches that I have had. And you want to know what the saddest part of the whole thing is?" I couldn't even answer her, I felt sick to my stomach so I just continued looking at her without saying a word. "I did nothing to stop it. I made excuses and the hospital truly believed I was the clumsiest person alive, when he actually took me to the hospital, that is."

I could feel my blood instantly boil with each word that was coming out of her mouth. At that very moment I wanted to go to the cemetery, pull that assholes body out of the grave, bring him back to life so I could beat the shit out of him then slowly and painfully kill him all over again. I couldn't believe someone could do all of that to this amazing woman. I reached over and laid my hand on top of hers. "Scotti, I don't know what to say. I'm so sorry."

She gave me a small smile, "Don't be sorry, Mason. I survived."

Yeah, she did. She survived abuse, only now to be starting another battle to survive. "How long did the abuse last?"

"Six years."

FUCK! "Six years? God Scotti, I…" I felt myself getting choked up and was afraid to say anything else.

"I kept telling myself I was going to get out of there but I had no friends, no family and no money. Sure, I could have run away but with absolutely no resources he would have found me, and things would have gotten so much worse. So, I just dealt with it… until that last night."

"What happened that last night?" I asked.

"It started the minute I woke up that morning. All I can think of was he was on drugs because even though he was abusive throughout our entire relationship, that day he seemed completely different. Anyway, I woke up and he was still asleep, or so I thought. As soon as I tried to get out of bed he grabbed me by my hair, pulled me back into the bed, tore my pajamas off and immediately began raping me. I screamed, scratched him, pulled his hair, nothing would get him to stop. It hurt so bad but he just wouldn't stop." She took a breath then continued. "Once he was done, I went into the bathroom to take a shower. I was so sore and everything, even water, hurt. As soon as I got out of the shower and walked into the bedroom he grabbed me and slammed me up against the wall and started punching me in my stomach, then my face. He tore the towel off of me, threw me on the ground and started raping me again." A couple of tears fell down her face and all I wanted in that very moment is for her to stop talking, but she was not done. "This happened for hours. By the time the day was over, I was in so much pain and had been raped at least five times but to be honest I lost count so it could have been more. I thought it was finally over so I slowly started making my way over to the bed so I could lie down. Well, he had other ideas. He came charging back in to the room then pushed me down and started slamming my head into the floor over and over again. I had not even had a chance to get dressed yet so there were no clothes to tear off of me. My only saving grace is that this was happening on his side of the bed and I knew he kept a gun in the drawer of his night stand because he held it to my head several times in the past. I don't know how it happened but a rush of adrenaline hit me and I knew I needed to do something drastic or I would not survive until the next day. I pushed him off of me, quickly jumped up, opened the drawer, grabbed the gun and pointed it at him. He didn't even seem fazed because he was coming right at me so I pulled the trigger without even thinking."

She stopped talking but I didn't need her to continue, I knew how this story ended. She was visibly shaken up and I was trying to hide how incredibly disturbed I was by her story but I don't think I was doing a great job of that. We both just sat in silence, neither of us knowing what to say to each other. I held her hand so she wouldn't think I was ready to jump up and run away but inside, I wanted to jump up and run away. Not because of her, but because I was feeling an anger inside that I have never in my life felt, and I didn't want her to see it.

"I know I probably gave you a lot more information than you wanted, but I needed you to know why I did what I did. I didn't want you to think badly of me." Her words were quiet and she was scared of my reaction.

"I know I haven't known you very long, but I don't think I could ever think badly of you. I will admit though, I am sick thinking about all of the shit that you had to go through. I wish there was something I could do to help you."

"You already did," she squeezed my hand a little tighter, "you let me talk and get all this out. Besides the police officer that came to my house that night, I have never told anyone that story."

I knew in that moment, that I wanted Scotti in my life. I not only felt comfortable just being around her but she obviously felt the same way.

"There is one more thing I need to tell you and I really hope this isn't the thing that is going to cause you to run."

I swallowed hard and my heart started beating faster. "You can tell me anything."

"After this all happened I was able to get in to the women's shelter and once I recovered from my injuries I was able to find a job. A few weeks later I was not feeling good, to the point where I couldn't hold any food down at all so the shelter supervisor had me take a pregnancy test and sure enough it came back positive." A couple of tears rolled down her cheek but she quickly wiped them away. "Three days later I had an abortion."

I was hurting for her but I would never run because of that, "Scotti, why would I possibly think badly about you because of that?"

She nodded her head but didn't really say anything at first then dropped her head, "I can't help but think that this cancer is punishment for my actions. Now, there is no way I can ever have a baby of my own."

I was glad the restaurant was mostly empty because Scotti's couple of tears turned into full on crying. I quickly moved to the chair next to her and pulled her into a hug. We sat like that, me holding her and her crying in my chest, for several minutes. She finally sat up and I picked up a napkin and gently wiped her face. I can't believe how much she has endured and it made me sick to my stomach that she could think for one minute that I would ever walk away from her because of everything she has told me. "I'm so sorry you not only had to go through that but go through all of that alone. I promise you, anything that comes up from here on out, you will not be going through alone." I gently kissed her tear stained cheek, "and don't ever think you are being punished. Your pregnancy was a result of an incredibly violent act. You did what you needed to do and I think you did the right thing."

She seemed surprised that I said that then got a smile on her face. I reached up and put my hand on her cheek and just held it there. Right as I started to pull away she placed her hand on top of mine to stop me. I stared into her eyes as she stared into mine and the next thing I knew she was slowly moving towards me. I knew she wanted to kiss me and I also knew I wanted nothing more than to kiss her back. Just before our lips met I stopped. "Scotti, are you sure?"

She smiled at me again, "I have never been more sure of anything in my entire life."

Just as the last word was out of her mouth, our lips met, into the most amazing kiss I have ever had. This was it… this was the moment that I knew I had fallen in love with this beautiful stranger.

Six

Scotti

I have never felt anything like this before. There were a million butterflies swimming around in my stomach, my whole body was weak, lips were tingling and… love? Is that possible? I just met Mason less than two weeks ago and have barely seen him since the day we met. How could I possibly be in love? It wasn't love, it was the feeling of being kissed for the first time in a very long time, that had to be it.

I never wanted this kiss to stop but we were in a restaurant so I know it couldn't go on forever. I pulled Mason closer to me and just as I did I heard someone clearing their throat. We both stopped and looked up at a waiter, who was looking extremely uncomfortable.

"I'm so sorry, but we are getting ready to close." He was shifting back and forth making me giggle, embarrassing him even more.

Mason reached into his back pocket, pulled out his wallet and handed over his credit card to the poor man, who practically ran away from us as soon as he had it in his hand. He turned back to me and smiled then leaned in and gave me another quick kiss. "I'm not ready to take you home," he said.

My whole body got a chill, but I wasn't scared, "I'm not ready for you to take me home, Mason," I told him.

"Scotti, I'm going to ask you something and I just want you to give me a completely honest answer."

I nodded nervously, "Okay."

"Will you stay with me tonight?"

I opened my mouth to speak but nothing came out. I wanted more than anything to stay with him but I also haven't been with a man in a couple of years and I admit, that part scared me. My hands started shaking and still nothing was coming out of my mouth.

"Fuck babe, I didn't mean to upset you. Nothing will happen that you don't want to happen. I just want you next to me, that's all, I promise."

I have never been able to trust anyone, man or woman, since everything happened with Charlie but I didn't get that feeling with Mason. The moment I saw him I felt in my heart that he was a good guy, not that I was ever a great judge of character since I thought Charlie was a great guy at first too. Something about Mason though, it gave me comfort, gave me hope for the future and that is something I have not had any of lately. My only hope was that I wasn't kidding myself. I can't go through another Charlie situation. I swallowed, took a deep breath and decided to follow my heart on this. "You didn't upset me. I would love to go home with you, Mason."

He grabbed my hand and jumped up, pulling me up with him just as the waiter walked back over with his credit card and the bill to sign. Mason quickly scribbled the tip and his signature on the receipt then we were practically running out the door to his truck. As soon as we both got inside he reached over and pulled me into another toe curling kiss, making what little bit of nervousness I had left inside of me disappear. "I know your past has left some pretty bad scars on you, both physically and mentally, but with your permission, I would love to show you that scars can be healed and that there are good men out there. I would like to show you that when a man touches you it doesn't have to hurt. I would like to show you that… you are loved."

I couldn't stop the tears that were falling down my face but for the first time in my life, these were happy tears. I don't know if I have ever shed happy tears before. "Mason," I was so afraid that I heard him wrong, "are you saying that you love me?"

He smiled at me, "Hell yeah I am. Is that completely crazy?" Before I could say anything he answered for me, "probably, but I don't care. When I kissed you in the restaurant I felt it and I don't care if I have known you for ten days or ten years, I am not going risk losing you because of a number."

It is completely crazy! There were still some things I needed to tell him but I didn't want to ruin this perfect moment, and what I had to say would definitely ruin it. "Mason, how can you possibly love me when we just met?" He opened his mouth like he was going to say something but I held my hand up to stop him, "That's a question I guess I need to ask myself too because, as completely insane and crazy as it is, I…" deep breath Scotti, you can do this, "love you too, Mason."

The smile that just went across Mason's face, because of me, is the best thing I have ever seen. He pulled me across the center console and on to his lap and I buried my face into his neck as he held me tight. In all of my twenty-eight years, I have never felt this way about anyone. Mason is right, who cares if we just met. If we feel it then we feel it and who gives a shit what anyone says. I don't know how far I am willing to go with Mason right now, but I do know that when the time comes, it won't be the painful experience I am used to. I can feel that Mason actually loves me and he is not just saying that to get me in bed. I hold him tight and can't let go, because once I tell him what I have been hiding from him, I am willing to bet he doesn't want anything more to do with me.

Seven

Mason

With the exception of my Mom, I have never in my life told a woman that I loved her, but I knew I couldn't go another second without saying it to Scotti. I never believed that a person could fall in love so quickly. If I am being honest, I am not sure I ever believed in love, but this crazy woman, who I saw for the first time while she was sitting on the beach crying, has made me a believer.

I could see in her eyes, when I asked her to stay with me, that she was a little frightened but I completely meant what I said. Nothing will happen that she doesn't want to happen. I just hate the thought of her going back to that women's shelter, where she has no friends and no family, when she could be in my arms tonight. She is starting chemo in a couple of days and I plan to talk to her about staying with me during her treatment. She is going to need help and I cannot imagine her getting much of it where she is currently living. We will discuss that later though; right now she is looking a bit overwhelmed.

I pull in to the driveway of my home and when I look over at Scotti she is staring out the window with wide eyes, "Holy shit Mason! I didn't realize you were so rich."

The fact that my small two-bedroom house that is in desperate need of a paint job, makes her believe that I am rich, makes me feel sad for her. She has endured way too much in her life but I am hoping that she can forget about all of that shit and just look towards our future.

"I am nowhere near rich babe. It's just a cozy little house." I don't want her to feel intimidated by anything of mine. I do well for myself but I don't live that way. Sure, I could have bought a much bigger house that doesn't need work done to it but I saw this one and immediately loved it. Besides it was just me so what would I need all of that space for?

Scotti smiles at me then slowly makes her way out of my truck. I jump out and meet her on her side then grab her hand and lead her up the creaky steps of my porch. I unlock the door but before I open it I turn to her. "Please tell me if anything about being here makes you uncomfortable and I will take you home," she nods her head, "I just wasn't ready for our night to end but I promise you, I have no expectations other than just wanting you next to me."

"Thank you," she said with a smile, "I admit, this is a little weird for me but it has nothing to do with you and everything to do with my life in general. In all the years I was with Charlie, he never once told me he loved me. All I ever wanted him to say is that he loved me but he never did. I have known you less than two weeks and you not only say you love me but I can actually feel in my heart that you really do love me and I know I love you too," she takes a deep breath, "I am just trying to wrap my head around everything right now."

Every time she tells me something about that piece of shit, I get more and more pissed off. He would repeatedly beat her, rape her, hurt her and all she wanted was for him to tell her he loved her. I can't imagine the strength it must have taken to pull that trigger on him but I almost wish she hadn't, so I could go and do it myself. Of course, her doing all of this has led me to her.

"Mason, are you okay?" She asked, pulling from my thoughts.

"Yes, of course. I was just thinking about everything you have been through."

"And let me guess, you are second guessing bringing me in to your life?" She said, with a little bit of sadness. How can she think I don't want her around because something that someone else has done to her in the past?

She turns towards the door and just before she reaches it she turns to me. "Thank you, Mason. Meeting you has been the best thing that has ever happened to me."

She turns around again and before she can even reach the door I am jumping in front of her to stop her. "Damn it, Scotti, you have got to stop running away from me!"

She looks down, almost embarrassed and when she looks up I can see the tears in her eyes but none are falling, "Sorry," she says softly.

"Why, Scotti? Why do you keep trying to run?"

She takes a deep breath. "Mason, these feelings I am having for you scare me. I have never before felt this way. I love you so much and I never want to be without you, but also, having me in your life means having drama. Not just because of my past but my present isn't too great either. I have a fight ahead of me and the last thing I want to do is drag you into it." Now the tears are falling. I reach out and pull her into a hug and kiss her head.

"Scotti, you are not drama, you are amazing. And as far as this fight… isn't it better to have someone by your side to fight it with you?"

She nods her head in my chest, "Yes."

We stay like that for a couple of minutes until Scotti pulls back, wipes her face with her hands then looks up at me. "Mason, my entire life I have been passed off, never loved, hell, never even been liked if I'm being honest. Then I met Charlie and I thought my luck had changed but that only lasted about five minutes. After everything was over with him I was still optimistic that someday, maybe, I would find someone that didn't despise me. Then this cancer shit happened and I just figured I was destined to be alone. I'm just scared."

I smile at her then place my palm on her cheek, "It scares me too. I have never felt this way about anyone before, but Scotti, this is real, I am real. I will never hurt you. When my hands touch you, it will never be out of anger or rage. I promise you that."

A couple more tears fell down her face but her smile makes it all worth it. "Thank you, Mason. I have never had anybody, and I do mean anybody, in my life until now." She looked down, took a deep breath then looked back into my eyes, "will you be my somebody?"

My heart was beating like it never has before. The chills running up and down my body was something I never felt. Scotti has made me feel things I never wanted to feel before so when she asked me that question there was no doubt about my answer, "With every sunrise and sunset that I am living and breathing, I will always be your somebody."

She quickly wrapped her arms around me tightly as I did to her and kissed her head. She lifted her head and gave me a soft kiss on the cheek. "Mason, there are still some things I need to talk to you about, some things that I can't keep from you, but for tonight, I just want to spend thinking of only us and not being sick, so I was wondering if… well, you can say no if you want to but… never mind."

She turned away, seemingly embarrassed, so I took her face in my hands and turned it back to me, "You can ask me anything, Scotti."

She looked down then looked back into my eyes, "Mason, will you make love to me?"

She was so scared to ask me that but I am so glad that she did. I have wanted to do nothing more than have her in my bed but I knew, with her, it had to be on her terms and I was completely okay with that. I lifted her up in to my arms and kissed her gently, "I can't imagine a better way to spend our evening than by making love to each other."

I slowly walked into my bedroom and gently set her on the bed. She was shaking but I could see how much she wanted this because I wanted it just as much, if not more. “Please don’t hurt me, Mason. For the first time in a long time, I feel safe,” she said almost in a whisper.

I kneeled down in front of her, pulled her face to mine and kissed her. “I promise that you are always safe with me.”

Eight

Scotti

I really surprised myself that I had the guts to ask Mason to make love to me, but with all this cancer shit happening to me lately, I have realized how short life can be and I decided to just do it. I was so worried he was going to laugh in my face or tell me he didn't want to do that with me but as soon as the question was out of my mouth and I saw the look on his face, I knew I had made the right decision in asking.

As he carried me into his bedroom, all I could think about was how safe I felt. It was a very foreign feeling to me but I loved it. Mason stood up, after assuring again me that he would never hurt me, and started slowly stripping off his shirt. I guess I need to do the same thing but as soon as I reach for the hem of my top, he stops me. "If you don't mind, I would love to be the one to remove that shirt from that beautiful body of yours," he said with a smile.

I dropped the shirt, then nervously put my hands in my lap and continued watching him as he removed all his clothes, down to just his boxer briefs. He reaches his hand out and pulls me up to stand in front of him. He softly kisses my lips then reaches down to the bottom of my shirt and slowly lifts it over my head, exposing my plain white bra that I got at a second-hand store. My embarrassment takes over and I quickly turn away from him and start heading towards the bathroom.

"Scotti, what's wrong? Did I hurt you?" Mason asked me in a panic.

I stop short of the bathroom door then shake my head and turn to him, "No, not at all. It's just…"

"Just what, baby?" He asked with concern.

I took a deep breath and slowly exhaled before I answered. "I just… I don't have sexy underwear and I'm embarrassed." I could feel my face getting hot and I felt like such an idiot worrying about stuff like that but I know guys really like those sexy bras and panties and I have never in my life owned anything beautiful like that.

Mason gives me a half smile and I know it's just a matter of time before he starts laughing at me. I am waiting for it but instead of laughing, he takes my face in his hands and looks into my eyes. "There is no amount of sexy underwear in the world that could make you look more beautiful than you already are. You are the sexiest woman I have even seen in my life and nothing you wear could make me feel any different, don't you understand that Scotti? I met you, was instantly attracted to you, fell in love with you and I did all of that before I ever saw your underwear. I don't need any of that to feel the way I feel about you."

He always knows exactly the right things to say to me to ease my mind and suddenly my plain, white, crappy bra doesn't seem so bad anymore. I reach back and unclasp it then slowly pull it down my arms and drop it to the floor. Mason takes a glance down at my breasts but quickly looks back into my eyes. That's just another reason why I have fallen for him, he is such a gentleman.

He reaches for the top button of my jeans, unbuttons them then slowly pulls the zipper down. I have nothing but boring plain white panties on but since we already had this discussion with my bra, I didn't even give a shit anymore.

He gently pulls my jeans down my legs and I grab on to his shoulders so I can step out of them. Once they are completely off, he throws them to the side then stands back up and pulls me into an intense kiss. Each kiss he gives me just gets better and better. I can't imagine what sex with him will be like and just the thought has made me wet. I want nothing more than to have Mason inside of me, but I am also afraid of going too fast. The last time I had sex was against my will and I don't want to get scared with Mason.

Mason pulls his lips from mine, leads me over to the bed, then gently lays me down and slowly pulls my panties off of me. He starts kissing my body, first my ankle, then up my leg, inner thigh, stomach, both breasts, neck then finally back on my lips again. He reaches over to the drawer of his nightstand and opens it, then pulls out a condom, causing me to freeze up. Mason has told me he wasn't looking for anything nor had he been with anyone in a very long time, so why did he have condoms in his drawer? He must sense my agitation because he immediately stops what he is doing.

"Okay, before you get upset, I bought these for you."

What the hell? "How is that even possible?"

He looked down, almost ashamed, "When I was out looking for you I knew that I would find you, I had no doubt. I stopped at the store one of the days to grab a few things and when I passed by the aisle with the condoms I grabbed a box. Maybe I was jumping the gun but for the first time in a long time I felt something and I knew I wanted this, with you and only you. I was not going to stop until I found you and I know it may sound dumb but I just knew we would end up together. I guess I wanted to be prepared," he shook his head and looked down embarrassed. "Wow! It sounds pretty fucking ridiculous when I say it out loud. Please don't be mad."

I felt a sense of relief and when I looked back into Mason's eyes, I realized he was probably thinking he just blew it. I admit, it did sound a little weird that while looking for me he felt the need to buy condoms. I touched the side of his face and smiled, "You're right, it does sound pretty ridiculous but I am not mad."

He chuckled and looked immediately relieved. He kissed me then took the condom, tore open the package and rolled it on. As soon as it was on, he positioned himself so the tip of his cock was barely touching me. "You still okay?" He asked me.

I nodded, "Never better."

Mason smiled then slowly started pushing himself inside of me. I know it sounds cliché but I literally think I saw fireworks. Having sex for me was always a painful and hateful experience. But the second Mason was inside of me, I realized that there was such a thing as love making and I knew, no matter what ever happened in my life, this moment was one I would never forget.

Nine

Mason

If there was ever any moment in my life that I can say, without a shadow of a doubt, that I felt at peace and happy, this would be that moment. I will admit, sex has been on my mind since the moment I met Scotti, but never in my life did I ever think it would feel like this. She has completely turned my life around in just the short time that I have known her and I can't even begin to imagine a world without her in it. She has quickly become my everything, and I am going to make sure I spend the rest of my life showing her just how much.

I am trying to make love to her as slow and gentle as I possibly can, knowing the trauma that she has suffered in the past, but she keeps grabbing my ass and pulling me closer to her, making it a lot more difficult to take my time. After the third time of her grabbing my ass, I can't take it anymore so I stop moving completely and stare into her eyes.

“Mason, what’s wrong?” She asks me, but instead of answering all I do is continue to stare. Her eyes start watering and she turns her face in embarrassment.

“Scotti, look at me.” I say to her, but she continues to look away. “Baby, please look at me.”

She slowly turns to look at me and when she does, one tear slowly rolls down her face, falling to the pillow under her head. “I am doing this all wrong, aren’t I?”

A few more tears fall down her face so I reach over and wipe them off, then lean my face into hers and lightly kiss her lips, “Babe, I promise you, you are doing everything right and if I made you feel differently, I am so sorry. I am just really trying so hard to do the right thing but I am afraid.”

She scrunches her forehead, “What do you mean doing the right thing? What are you afraid of?”

“Hurting you and causing you pain. I don’t ever want you to feel like you did before,” I take a deep breath, “I don’t want you to look at me and see him.” At that moment, I felt like I was the one that was going to start crying. I can’t begin to imagine what Scotti went through during that time with Charlie but if she ever looked at me with fear like I imagine she did with him, I don't think I could ever survive that.

Scotti reaches up and rubs my cheek, "God, Mason, do you really think I could ever see you as evil like that. Since meeting you, I am the happiest I have ever been in my entire life. I would never have let you kiss me, let alone make love to me if I ever saw you as anything more than perfect. I am sorry if I ever gave you that impression."

"You didn't. It wasn't that. It's just, when we are making love and you are grabbing me, I want to start moving faster but I don't know what is too fast and what is not or what will hurt you or what won't."

She smiles at me, with that smile that constantly melts my heart, "Mason, I wanted you to move faster, that was the point of me grabbing you."

"I am scared of hurting you." I tell her.

"I trust you, Mason. I know you would never hurt me."

"You're right, I never would. I am just worried after everything that has happened to you that I may do it unintentionally." Between her traumatic past and her recent surgery I don't know what I can and can't do. I want this to be perfect for her.

"Okay, let me make this as clear as I possibly can so you won't worry anymore," she reached out and grabbed my ass again. "I want you to fuck me like you have never fucked another woman before. I want you to make me scream until I no longer have a voice. I want you to make me come, multiple times I might add then I want to fall asleep in your arms, wake up in the morning and do it all over again." She raised one eyebrow, "is that okay?"

Holy fuck! All I could do is swallow then stare at her with my mouth wide open like an idiot. My already hard cock just got even harder to the point that it was almost painful. Scotti started laughing at me as I was still trying to process what she just said.

She started snapping her fingers in front of my face, "Mason, did I scare the shit out of you?"

Finally, I was able to find my voice, "Um, no, sorry. I am just trying to figure out if you really said all of that or if I just had a really short, really incredible dream."

She smiled widely then giggled, "I said it, and I mean it. Maybe shit happened in my past but I refuse to let that asshole scare me away from the best thing that has ever happened to me. I don't want you to be afraid of me of hurting me. I promise you, if I am uncomfortable with anything, I will let you know."

I know that I am the luckiest fucker to ever walk the face of this Earth and if I hadn't already fallen for Scotti, I would have for sure at this very moment. I bring her face to mine in a kiss that is so hot I feel like I can come from just that alone. I start moving again, making us both moan loudly. "Holy hell, baby," was all I could say.

She was moaning and the sweat was starting to build up between us, making our bodies incredibly slick. I have never felt anything so amazing before in my life. "Please Mason, don't stop, this feels so good."

That just kicked my body into high gear and I started moving even faster. I couldn't get enough of her. I could tell by the look on her face that she was close to an orgasm, which was a good thing considering I was about to come any minute. "Mason! OH GOD!" She screamed, arching her back digging her nails into my skin. I kept going at a quick pace which was making Scotti moan and yell even louder and just as she reached down and grabbed my ass again, I came with a vengeance. "FUCK!" I yelled just as Scotti let out another scream, having her second orgasm.

I continued moving inside of her but slower and slower until I stopped completely. I laid on top of her, still inside her, while both of us were breathing like we had just run a 10 mile marathon. After catching my breath a little I lifted my head and saw the most beautiful sight I have ever seen; Scotti, and those beautiful blue eyes and that beautiful smile on her face that I have fallen in love with this past week. "How do you feel?" I asked her as I leaned in and gently kissed her lips.

She kissed me back then smiled again, "Incredible. I have never felt anything so wonderful in my life. Thank you, Mason."

I smiled at her again, "What can you be thanking me for? We both did this and I don't know about you but I am thinking we are pretty fucking phenomenal together."

She let out a little giggle then rubbed her hand down my back, "I am thanking you because that was the first time I have ever had sex because I wanted to. I didn't realize it could feel so amazing."

My heart immediately dropped from my chest and my jaw dropped. I know she said that Charlie raped her but I was under the impression that they had a relationship in the beginning. "What? I thought the two of you were a couple?"

She shook her head, "He wined and dined me, we kissed but that was it. The first time we had sex was the first time I had ever had sex in my life. I was scared and he was being sweet and loving in the beginning but when it got time to actually doing it, I got scared and asked him to stop. Well, let's just say he didn't stop and it was the most painful moment of my life."

Fucking dick! I already hated that asshole but he fucking raped her their very first time… HER very first time! I jumped up and started pacing the room, not caring that I was completely naked. "Shit, Scotti, why would you stay with him after he did that to you?" I yelled, immediately feeling like a piece of shit.

She sniffled like she was holding in sobs but she wasn't letting any tears fall, "Because, I had nowhere else to go, Mason!" She yelled back, then lowered her voice, "I know that makes me weak but I seriously had nowhere else to go and I just couldn't live on the streets anymore, so I took whatever he dealt me, just so I wouldn't be alone."

I quickly walked back over to the bed and pulled her in to me so tight that I thought I might break her, but I couldn't let go. Scotti was incredible and loving and this fucking prick took advantage of that. At that moment, I felt a tear roll down my cheek and on to the top of Scotti's head. I kissed her head, then down to her cheeks, and finally her lips. "You are always safe with me. You will never be treated like that ever again for as long as we live. I love you Scotti. I don't give a fuck if I just met you, I love you so much and there will never be any doubt in your mind how much I do, I promise you that."

She smiled at me, put her arms around me then buried her face in my neck, "Thank you Mason. I love you too, for the rest of my life." She lifted her head and a strange look crossed her face but it quickly disappeared.

"I have never had a relationship before and what we just did is something that I have never felt in all my years," I admitted. "What I am trying to say is that, as far as I am concerned, this is my first time. Nothing and nobody existed before the day I met you."

Scotti had tears in her eyes and was smiling at me. She gave me a gentle kiss then smiled again, "Then you are my first too, Mason. I don't even remember what happened before I met you."

I smiled at her, then we kissed until our lips started going numb. We laid on the bed, face to face, holding each other until Scotti could no longer hold her eyes open. Once they were closed and her breathing evened out, I let out a huge breath that I had been holding in. I have never been one to dream of one day having that family but everything changed with Scotti. She shines a light in my life after years of it being so dark. She has a fight ahead of her but I have no doubt in my mind, she and I will be growing old together.

Ten

Scotti

Mason was sound asleep and as much as I wanted to just lay here and watch him, I really wanted to surprise him and cook breakfast for him. I quietly got out of bed, careful not to wake him, crept out of the room and into the kitchen and got started. It felt weird going through his cabinets but there was no way I had time to walk to the store, get everything we needed for breakfast then get back before he woke up. Besides, the last thing I wanted is for Mason to open his eyes, see me gone and think I bailed on him after the amazing night we had.

I had the eggs in a bowl and started whisking them with a fork when I felt two incredibly strong arms wrap around my waist, "Good morning beautiful," Mason said in my ear, then squeezed me tighter and kissed my cheek. I stopped whisking, set the bowl on the counter then turned around and immediately planted my lips on his. Who needs eggs when I have these sexy as hell arms around me and these lips on mine?

"Mmmmm," I moaned, not able to get any words out. We continued kissing, Mason pushing his tongue into my mouth, me doing the same, until he reached down, grabbed my legs and lifted me on to the kitchen counter.

He pulled his mouth from mine and was breathing heavy, as was I. "Fuck babe, I can't control myself around you."

I smiled at him, feeling the exact same way, "Please don't."

Mason lifted me from the counter and I wrapped my legs around his waist as he practically ran over to the couch. He laid me down then stood up and pulled his shirt and shorts off, showing off his incredible body. Apparently, I was not getting my clothes off fast enough because as I was pushing my panties off, Mason moved my hands away then practically ripped them in half to remove them. He then grabbed the hem of my shirt, yanked it over my head and tossed it aside. Before it even hit the floor, Mason was inside of me, making me cry out.

Mason stopped immediately, "Shit, Scotti, I am so sorry. I got carried away." Mason said, mistaking my cry as painful instead of what it really was… fucking incredible.

"Holy hell, Mason that was not a bad sound! Don't stop!" I yelled. He had a look of relief on his face then immediately started moving again. I wrapped my legs around his waist which made him start moving even more. This felt so good. I knew that I was not going to last long but instead of fighting it, I let myself go with a scream that probably woke every one of Mason's neighbors. Before I had even finished my orgasm, he was having one and his yell definitely put mine to shame.

Everything happened so quickly and it took me a minute to wrap my brain around everything. "If making eggs gets me this kind of reaction, I am going to make sure I make them every fucking day of my life!" I said, once I was finally able to catch my breath, rewarding me with a full belly laugh from Mason that I have not yet heard.

"Just you breathing turns me on," he said with a smile, "I'm sorry if I ruined your breakfast."

I pretended to contemplate what he was saying, "You should be sorry. Eating was so much more exciting than what we just did. Please don't let it happen again."

Mason smiled at me the proceeded to squeeze my side, causing me to squirm. "You are such a smart ass," he said to me, continuing to tickle me.

Once he realized just how ticklish I was, he decided to keep going, making me laugh so hard I was losing my breath. "Mason, stop, please!" I yelled, but he would not stop and I was getting to the point of being sick from it. I always hated being tickled but when Mason started doing it, I figured it would be fun. Now I just wanted it to stop. I begged again for him to stop, but he just kept tickling and wouldn't stop so I did the next thing I could think of. I punched him directly in his nose, putting an immediate stop to it.

He reached up to his nose to check if it was bleeding, which it wasn't, "Did you just punch me?" He asked me in shock.

I took a couple of deep breaths, still trying to recover, "Yes. I am so sorry Mason but you just wouldn't stop and I didn't know what else to do." I really did feel bad for punching him.

At first I thought he was mad at me because he wasn't saying anything but then he smiled. "You just punched me in the nose and all I can think about is how incredibly turned on I am right now."

"Me kicking your ass is a turn on?"

He laughed, "I wouldn't go as far as to say you kicked my ass, but yeah, that was pretty sexy."

I thought that meant he was ready for round two, but instead he climbed off of me then lifted me so I was straddling him, kissed me, then I laid my head on his chest, listening to his heartbeat. We were both completely naked and I don't know about Mason, but I was completely content. I lifted his hand to my lips and gave it a gentle kiss. "Sorry for kicking your ass."

He laughed as he shook his head, but didn't disagree with me. Suddenly his smile quickly went away and he had a look of fear on his face, "Fuck, Scotti. I didn't use a condom!"

I hadn't even thought of that either. "Are you clean?" I asked him.

"Babe, of course, it has been years since I have been with anyone, I told you that."

That made me smile, "After everything that happened with… well, you know who… I had every test under the sun and have not been with anyone else and of course you already know there is no way for me to get pregnant so I think we are good."

He slowly nodded his head then I leaned in and kissed him. "I want you so bad right now." He talks like we didn't just finish having sex.

My kisses turned more passionate but I quickly pulled away from him and jumped off his lap, "Well, I guess I better get working on those eggs."

"Seriously? You are standing here, completely naked, after having mind blowing sex and I just told you how much I want you, and you are thinking about eggs?"

He was right, that was incredibly mind blowing sex but instead of agreeing with him I smiled and decided to mess around with him, "Yeah, well I don't know if I would call that mind blowing. I mean, it was alright."

His mouth dropped open and he had a look on his face of someone that had just lost his puppy and I was doing everything I could not to laugh. "It was just alright?" He asked.

I shrugged my shoulders, "Yeah, I mean, I liked it and all. I guess I thought you would do better."

I think I went too far with my joke because his mouth fell open even more. I turned to walk towards the kitchen, more so he wouldn't see my face trying to hold in a smile, but only made it two steps before I was being picked up, making me scream. "Mason, what are you doing?"

"Showing you just how much better it could really be!" He yelled as he was running with me in his arms. As soon as we got in the bedroom we were on the bed and Mason was inside of me before I could blink twice. I didn't think it could be better than what we just had on the couch, but he showed me just how much better it could be… God did he ever!

Eleven

Mason

Today is Scotti's first day of chemo and I am not sure who is more scared. Actually, I know who is since Scotti is acting like we are taking a trip to the grocery store or something, although watching her, I can tell that she is starting to get a little nervous. How could she not? She is having poison pumped into her body, at least that is how she describes it. Once we get to the doctor's office, Scotti signs in then we sit hand in hand in the waiting area. My leg is bouncing so she reaches her hand over to stop it. "Mason, stop, you are freaking me the hell out."

"I'm sorry, I'm just nervous for you. The thought of you going through this is not something that sits well with me."

She takes a deep breath then nervously smiles at me, "Mason, before we go back, there is something I need to tell you…"

"Scottlyn Marks!" Her name is called and we both jump up and walk towards the nurse and into the back rooms. There are a few people, sitting in recliner chairs with bags of the liquid medicine hooked up to them. Some are sleeping, a couple are reading, and a couple look at us as we walk by. We get inside an empty room where the nurse takes all of Scotti's vitals then informs us that the doctor will be in to talk to us in a few minutes.

Scotti nods at the nurse, "Thank you." She takes a deep breath and that is when I can really see the nerves come out. I think being back here and seeing everyone having their treatment is starting to hit her.

After the nurse leaves, I sit next to Scotti right as she turns to me, "Mason, there really is something I need to talk to you about that is very important but every time I try, we get interrupted. Maybe you should go wait in the waiting room while I do this, then we can go somewhere and talk after I am done."

"No way babe, I promised you I am not leaving your side and I meant it. We will talk when you are done, with no interruptions, I promise."

She takes in a deep breath then slowly lets it out, "Okay, but there is something I need to at least tell you before the doctor comes in."

I lift her hand up to my mouth and kiss it, "Of course, you can tell me anything."

"Well…"

"Scotti, how are you feeling today?" The doctor says as he walks in, shakes Scotti's hand then turns to me, "I am assuming you are the boyfriend."

I smile, loving the sound of that, "Yes sir, I am Mason Shaw." I reach out and we both shake hands.

Dr. Hammond sits down and starts looking through, what I assume is Scotti's file, and then closes it. "Okay Scotti, so as we discussed at your last appointment, we are hoping to slow down the cancer spreading with this chemo, but unfortunately that is the best we can do."

"Wait, what did you just say?" I ask, interrupting the doctor but hoping that I just heard him completely wrong.

He looked over at Scotti, seeking her approval to continue. She takes a deep breath then nods her head so the doctor turns to talk to me, "Mr. Shaw, once we found out that the cancer had spread…"

I am not sure what he said after that. I am feeling like the room is spinning and a nauseous feeling hits me so hard that I feel like I am going to pass out.

"…so Scotti decided that palliative chemotherapy is the way to go." I hear the doctor say, missing most of what he just said.

What the fuck is happening here? I am so confused right now and I want to ask questions but I can't seem to get any words out.

Dr. Hammond turns back to Scotti, "So, I just want to make sure this is something you are prepared for again before we get started with everything," he says.

Scotti isn't saying a word. She is staring at me and tears are falling down her face but she isn't saying a fucking word, "Wait a minute!" I yell to the doctor then turn to Scotti. "What is he talking about? Why is he saying that your cancer has spread?"

She is crying but she still isn't saying anything so I look over at the doctor, who looks stunned by my outburst but is no longer talking, so I look back at Scotti, "Babe, please, what is going on here? What does palliative mean?"

Scotti wipes the tears from her eyes and takes a deep breath, "Palliative chemo is chemo that can possibly shrink the cancer which in turn can possibly prolong my life a little."

"So, it can still cure you, right?"

She shakes her head as the tears start falling at a rapid pace, "No," she says sadly, "I can't be cured, Mason. Unfortunately my cancer is terminal."

I felt nothing, absolutely nothing. The numbness inside of me was something that I never even knew existed, not even when I lost my parents. Scotti and I are supposed to grow old together, but instead I am being told that she is only pumping this poison in her body to give her a little extra time in life. "When you say prolong your life, exactly how much more time is this going to give you?"

She puts her head down and lets a few more tears fall, "Not much. Maybe a few months, maybe not. It's not really something the doctors can determine."

My confusion has now turned to anger and I jump out of my chair, "Then why the fuck are you putting yourself through this?"

She snaps her head up at me, "WHAT? Are you fucking serious? Let me see Mason, maybe because I am not ready to die yet!"

"But if you are dying anyway, why would you put your body through this?" As I am asking her this I am confusing the shit out of myself. Why the hell am I fighting her on doing whatever it takes to live a little longer? What is making me even angrier is why the hell she did not tell me all of this before!

I turn to say something else and Scotti puts her hand up, "I am sorry for not telling you all of this sooner, that was wrong of me, but I have known you for about a minute, Mason. You don't get to dictate what I am doing here. I know you are probably wondering why someone with the shitty life that I have wants to live longer, but I was not ready to leave it yet, okay?"

That was not at all what I was thinking but I can see where I might have led her to believe that. Just as I started to protest, she continued, "Chemo sucks, it going to make me sicker than a dog and I will lose my hair but you know what? Being sick and losing my hair means I am still alive!"

My heart breaks for her at that very moment. Dying scares her so much that she will put herself through the hell of chemotherapy just so she can stay alive a little bit longer. I feel like the biggest fucking asshole on the planet right now. I step towards Scotti because at this point all I want to do is wrap my arms around her, but she immediately pushes me away. "You need to leave, Mason."

"What?"

"GET. OUT!" She yells then turns and walks over to the window with her back facing me.

I walk up behind her but don't touch her, "Scotti, I'm sorry. Please don't push me away. I want to be here with you."

She turns around and there are no longer just a couple of tears falling down her face, there is a whole river of them. "Well I don't want you here. I had every intention of doing this alone so that's what I'm going to do."

"Scotti, don't do this. I love you and you love me too."

She stands there for a few seconds not speaking but when she does, my broken heart all but dies at that moment. "No, I don't love you. I never loved you and I don't want you here."

I stand there in shock, not knowing what to say to her. I know we just met but what we have is real, at least it felt like it to me, "You're lying." I tell her.

She takes a deep, shaky breath, "No, I'm not. You were nice to me, it felt good to get some attention and you said you loved me so I said it back just so you would continue spending time with me. I didn't mean it though," she swallows roughly, "how could I love someone I just met? That is just ridiculous."

I want to believe that she is lying but each word that comes out of her mouth makes me believe she is being completely truthful, and that hurts more than I could ever imagine. My feet are planted to the floor. I don't want to leave her. No matter what she just said to me, I still love her.

Dr. Hammond clears his throat, reminding us that he is still in the room. "Scotti, I am sorry but we really need to get going on this, I have other patients that I need to see." He says.

She finally tears her eyes away from me and looks at him, "Of course, I'm so sorry." Then she turns back to me, "thanks for bringing me, but I've got it from here."

I walk up to her until we are toe to toe. Since she is shorter than me, she has to look up but she isn't pushing me away. I bring my hands to each side of her face, pull her face to mine and gently kiss her lips, "Everything I have said to you has been completely true and even if you don't love me, I will always love you. Nothing will ever change that, Scotti."

I back away but not before I see her try to hide the tear that falls down her face. I turn to the door, hoping and praying that she will stop me, but she never does. I open it and turn back to Scotti, who still has not moved an inch. Instead of telling her again that I love her, I turn around and walk out the door, leaving not only the woman I love to fight this alone, but my heart completely crushed, on the floor next to her feet.

Twelve

Scotti

All I could do was stare at the closed door. I am not a liar. I usually tell it like it is with no regrets but today I lied.

I lied to Mason.

I do love him.

I am in love with him.

I will never stop loving him.

He is the best thing that I have ever had in my life and I not only hurt him but I just let him walk out the door. I don't know how much more time I have on this Earth but I do know it isn't long. Do I want to chase after him, bring him into this for him to have to say goodbye to me in a few months? I just can't do it. I know I should have pushed him away before either of us had the chance to grow feelings for each other but it felt so good to have someone, even if it was just for a very short amount of time.

To love and to be loved in return is the best feeling I have ever had in my entire life.

I regain my composure, then look over to Dr. Hammond and give him a nod to let him know I am ready. As I sit down on the chair to discuss my treatment, I say a silent prayer that once Mason calms down, he will forgive me. I don't want to die knowing the only man I ever loved now hates me.

Thirteen

Mason

Falling off the wagon didn't work the way I was hoping it would. Before I got sober, I drank to forget. I drank to feel nothing. I drank so I could actually sleep. This time, I didn't forget, I felt every bit of hurt and I have barely slept a wink. It has been a week since Scotti kicked me out of her doctor's office and the only things I have been able to do is drink and miss her like crazy. The hurt that I felt when she told me she didn't love me, was something I have never felt before. I didn't even know this kind of pain existed.

I have been to the women's shelter where Scotti is living, several times in fact, trying to get her to talk to me but they won't let me in to see her. I have stood outside screaming her name, begging her to come outside and talk to me but all I got was threatened with the cops being called on me. She is suffering alone and it's killing me. I should be there to hold her hair back while she is sick. I should be there to put the cool rag on her head when she is so hot she is sweating profusely. I should be there to hold her while she has the chills and is crying from the pain of the drugs in her body. It should be me! Not people at a shelter who don't give two shits about her!

Not feeling in the mood to be around anyone today, I decided drinking on the beach was a good idea. There is about 45 minutes left before sunset, Scotti's favorite time of day, so I decide to torture myself even more and watch it while thinking of her, and missing the hell out of her. Of course, there really isn't a time of the day that I am not.

As I sit, or more like fall, on to the sand, all I can think about is the day I met her here and how sad she looked and how, even though I just met her, all I wanted to do was kiss her. I take a giant swig of my beer and just as I am going to set it down, a person stands right in front of me, blocking my view of the water and pissing me the hell off.

"Do you mind getting the fuck out of my way?" I slur, without even looking up.

"Yes, actually I do mind." That voice startles me but also something inside of me angers. When I lift my head, I see Scotti standing there with her hands on her hips.

"Scotti, if you are here to make me feel shittier than I already do then you can fucking leave!" I yell. I missed her so much and now she is right in front of me and I am being an asshole.

She falls down to her knees right in front of me and when I look into her scared and sad eyes, my anger is replaced with sadness. I want to grab her and kiss her, but instead, I sit there staring into her eyes and not speaking a word.

"Mason, I just need to say something to you and after I am done, if you still want me to leave, then I will leave and never say another word to you. I promise."

The thought of never hearing from her again makes me immediately sick so I nod my head, letting her know to continue.

She takes a deep breath then lets it out, "I have never lied in my life. If I would have just lied to Charlie when he asked me if I loved him or when he asked me how much I liked being fucked by him, I probably would have had a lot less beatings, but I didn't." Her bringing up Charlie, when I am drunk as hell and feeling like shit, makes the vomit start rising in my throat but I let her continue. "Like I said, I have never lied before… until that day in the doctor's office."

Scotti has tears running down her face and I could tell she was having a hard time speaking so I reached over and grabbed her hand, making her smile. It was a weak smile but at least it was a smile. "What did you lie about?" I asked her quietly.

"Mason, I lied when I told you that I didn't love you," she let go of my hand and wiped her face, then laid it back in mine, "I love you so much. I loved you before you even told me you loved me. I was upset and scared standing there in that office and I realized that starting a relationship with you right now was a terrible idea. I am going to die, there is nothing anyone can do to save me. I was selfish for letting you in but nobody in my entire life has ever made me feel as special and as loved as you have. I just wanted to feel that connection to someone but in the meantime, I should have told you how bad the cancer was, so you could have chosen if I was someone that you wanted to give your time to, knowing that I wouldn't be around for long."

I hate to admit it, but I stopped listening after she told me that she loved me. Those three little words literally made my broken heart feel whole again. They gave me a relief that I needed more than anything. I reached out for her and pulled her until she was sitting on my lap then slammed my lips in to hers and kissed the shit out of her. I know she is dying, I know I won't have her to grow old with, but I will be damned if I lose out on what little time we do have with each other. I stop kissing her and pull her close to me and hold her. I never ever want to let her go.

I am keeping her held tightly. I can't seem to let go. I want to lie her down, right here in the sand, and make love to her so badly but I remember something and immediately lift my head to look at her. "Fuck, Scotti, how are you feeling? I should have asked that sooner, I am so sorry. I don't know much about chemo but you seem to be taking it pretty well."

She looked down in sadness, "That is actually something else I was going to talk to you about," she takes a deep breath then continues, "I have done a lot of thinking about this since that day in the doctor's office. I have given a lot of thought to whether or not I want that drug going through my system and making me sick just to die anyway. I don't want to spend my last day's sick," she looked back in to my eyes, "I don't have much time, but I decided I wanted to spend the time I did have doing what I want. So, I decided against doing the chemo, and I am just going to let the cancer run its course."

And just like that, my heart once again shattered. I saw our time together become even shorter and in that moment, for the first time since I can remember, I dropped my head, and I cried.

Fourteen

Scotti

When a person is told that they are dying, there is so much that goes through their head. In most cases, at least from what I was told, the first thing they think about is their families and loved ones. Well, when I was told I was dying, I didn't even have a friend, let alone any family. I thought of only myself. I was wishing I had someone other than myself to think of. I was wishing that someone would be there to hold my hand and tell me we would get through this together. Now that I have that person, I'm not so sure I feel that way any longer.

I now have someone else to think of and I have someone that will be holding my hand through this and I have someone, sitting in front of me with tears rolling down his face, because I am dying and you know what? IT. FUCKING. SUCKS! The reality of what is happening just escalated with the first tear that fell down Mason's cheek. I am now leaving someone behind that is going to be heartbroken and sad and I don't like this feeling one bit. After spending all these months envying all these people that have families to love them and support them through this, I am now regretting every bit of that.

I love Mason, more than I ever thought I could love someone, especially someone that I haven't known for long. I can't imagine not having that amazing first week with him but I now wish I never met him. It breaks my heart to say that, but it's true. If we would have never met, he would be living his life just the way he was before he met me, not thinking about his dying girlfriend. I want to stand up, give him one last kiss and run away so fast but the fact of the matter is, Mason isn't going anywhere. He is going to see my life slowly fade away. He is going to see me get to a point where I can no longer eat. He is going to see me not be able to get out of bed. He is going to see me take my last breath. He is going to have to learn to survive… without me.

I reach up and wipe the tears from his face, "Mason, I'm sorry. You shouldn't have to be dealing with any of this." I tell him truthfully. He decided to change up his running routine one day and now Hurricane Scotti has entered his life.

He leans in to me and kisses the palm of my hand. His tears have slowed down but there are still a few rolling down his cheeks, "there is nowhere I would rather be than with you right now. This past week without you has been the worst week I have ever had in my life. I missed you so much."

I smile at him, feeling the same exact way, "I missed you too. I'm so sorry for everything I said to you at Dr. Hammond's office."

He shakes his head, "Let's not even talk about that anymore. It was a minor setback. All I want to focus on is you and me."

"Are you sure you want this Mason?" Although I am asking, it would break my heart if he decided to just walk away.

"Do I want to lose you? Fuck no! I am sick just thinking about it. If I learned anything this past week it is how much time I don't want to lose with you anymore. I want to touch you every chance I get. I want to kiss your lips and feel your arms around me. I want to watch your hair blow in the breeze while we are sitting here watching the sunset. I want to memorize everything I can about you because, before I know it, those memories will be all I will have left of you," he squeezes my hand then kisses it. "If I was told I only had five minutes with you, I wouldn't take my eyes off you the entire time, in hopes that your face and your smile become burned into my brain permanently. You may physically be leaving but until the day I die, you will be in my heart and I will never, ever let you go."

Now I am the one that is crying. I don't know where I am going, but I would like to believe that there is a Heaven and I think I deserve to be there, but until I take my last breath I am going to pray, that wherever I end up, my memory of Mason will never fade away.

"OK Mason, we have something else very important to talk about." I tell him, as we are walking across the parking lot to get inside his truck. After everything that happened at the beach, we did some hugging, lots of kissing, watched the sunset, then both decided we needed food. All the crying has made us both hungry so now we are heading to get Chinese food at his favorite restaurant.

"What else could we possibly talk about that we haven't already said this afternoon?" He asks me just as we reach his truck.

I hold my hand out to him, "Keys, now." I say to him seriously.

"What are you talking about?"

"When I ran into you, you were drinking. Not just drinking a little. You were drunk. I am not getting in a car with you after you were just drunk on the beach a couple short hours ago. I may be dying but I don't have a death wish. If you want me to go anywhere with you, you will hand me your keys and let me drive, or we can walk, you decide."

He drops his head, reaches in his pocket and grabs his keys, "I'm so sorry," he says quietly as he hands me the keys.

"You don't have to be sorry Mason, just please don't do that again," I reach up and place my hand on his cheek. "You told me how hard it was to get sober and I don't want you to ever go back to that dark place."

He leans in and kisses me gently on the lips, "I won't ever do it again."

"Promise?"

"I promise you, babe."

I take a deep breath, "Not even after I die?"

His eyes immediately well up with tears. It takes him a minute to regain his composure, "I promise, not even after you die," he says quietly.

He puts his arms around me and pulls me into his chest tightly, resting his chin on top of my head. I reach my arms around him and hold him, so happy to feel his body again, "I love you Mason."

He kisses the top of my head, "I love you too Scotti, always and forever."

We stay like that for several minutes, neither of us wanting to let go. Once we finally do, Mason opens the drivers' side door for me. I meant what I said about not getting in the car with him but now that I am the one sitting behind the wheel, I am wishing we would have walked. I have my license but I can't even remember the last time I actually drove. Mason hops in the truck and looks over at me with a smile, "Let's get out of here, I'm starving," he says, oblivious to my impending panic attack.

As soon as I start it up, my heart immediately begins racing. If I can get us to the restaurant in one piece, it's going to be a miracle. I grab my seatbelt and fasten it quickly, "Mason, put your seatbelt on please," I tell him.

He looks over at me smiling, "You planning on crashing my truck?"

I just look at him then turn to face forward.

"Scotti?" He says my name slowly but I don't answer. I slowly pull out of the parking lot, hoping and praying that I don't damage anything in my path.

Fifteen

Mason

Note to self: Never, ever do anything stupid that makes it so Scotti has to drive. I have seen some bad drivers before but this girl takes the cake. I literally saw my life flash before my eyes at least four times during the fifteen minute drive to the restaurant. It feels like everything around me is spinning but the good thing is, I am positive that I am one hundred percent sober now.

We are sitting in my truck in the parking lot of the restaurant but I can't seem to move. I almost feel paralyzed.

"Mason? Are you okay?" Scotti puts her hand on my leg, pulling me out of my thoughts.

I look over at her wide eyes, "Scotti, I have made it clear how much I love you, right?"

She nods her head wide eyed and swallows, "Yes," she says quietly.

"Then when I say that you are the worst fucking driver I have ever met in my life, you know I say that out of love, right?"

She smiles then lets out a giggle, "I never said I was a good driver."

"You never said you were a shit driver either! Do you think you can warn me next time?" I said completely serious. I grabbed the keys from her and stick them in my pocket, "Never mind, there will NEVER be a next time."

Scotti's giggle turns into a full-blown laugh causing me to start laughing until we are both crying from the laughter. "This should teach you to keep your stupid ass sober from now on." Scotti says while still laughing, making me laugh even more.

"Fuck, babe, I don't even want to see alcohol anymore after this, let alone drink it. You almost hit an old lady with a walker!"

"Hey, that was not my fault, she got in my way!" Scotti says smiling, but looking like she truly believes that, which scared me even more.

"In your way? Scotti, she was on the fucking sidewalk! How did she get in your way?"

"She just did, ok?" She was mock pouting so I reached over and smashed her face into mine and kissed her hard. She resisted, for about two seconds then she pushed her tongue into my mouth, making me hard, and no longer hungry for Chinese food. We kissed and kissed and didn't stop until we had no choice because we couldn't catch our breath.

"First my cooking is a turn on and now my driving? Hand over those keys because I need to circle the block," she said, laughing.

I immediately shook my head, "Oh hell no! No way, no how, not ever again!"

Scotti started giggling, "Okay, no more. Now, can we please eat? I am starving and after that kiss I need to gain my strength for what I am hoping is to come later," she said, blushing.

Damn that woman knew how to get to me, "Don't worry babe, there will be lots to come later."

I jumped out of the car then ran over to her side just as she was stepping out. She closed her door then we walked hand in hand into the restaurant. Dinner needed to get done quickly, I had a lot of making up to do tonight, and I plan on making up with Scotti multiple times.

As much as it pained me to know Scotti wasn't going to be in my life for much longer, I can honestly say that during dinner I didn't think about her cancer one time. We laughed so much and talked about everything under the sun. I thought our first date was amazing but this one just topped that by a mile. Instead of telling each other our sad stories of our shitty lives, we talked about stupid shit like funny movies we like or weird things we did growing up. I felt like I have known her for years. I had a crazy idea cooking in my brain but I wasn't going to let her know what I was thinking just yet. I wanted us to have tonight. After the way I talked to her at the hospital she deserved tonight. Tomorrow, when we wake up, I will tell her my idea. It's crazy, it's insane but like we have both said about everything else, it's us. Now, I just hope she will go along with it.

Sixteen

Scotti

I always wondered if you could miss things after you die. Like, will I miss my pillow on my bed that is by far the most comfortable pillow I have ever laid my head on? Or will I miss the hot Chai Tea Latte at Starbucks? Since the day I was diagnosed with cancer, I always wondered those things. Now I am sitting here, watching Mason concentrate on the road as he drives us to his house, and wondering if it's possible to miss things after I die. If it is, I know Mason will be the number one thing I will miss. I have read books and watched movies about people falling in love quickly and always thought it was such bullshit. Not anymore. Now I know it is so real. Now I know that I can find someone and know immediately that they belong in my life.

Instead of feeling blissful and happy, I am starting to feel angry. Actually, angry isn't the right word. Now I am feeling fucking pissed! Why did I have to find Mason when I was at the end of my life? Why couldn't I find him years ago, before I ever met Charlie? I clinch my fists and turn my head towards the window, not wanting to show Mason how pissed off I am. We continue driving another ten minutes or so and as soon as we stop in his driveway I jump out of the car and quickly start walking down the street.

"Scotti, where are you going?" Mason yells after me.

I couldn't answer, instead I walk at a faster pace but my short legs are no match to Mason's long legs so before I know it, his big arms are wrapping around me to stop me.

"Mason, please let me go." I whisper to him.

"Scotti, if there is one thing you have not figured out yet, it is that I will never, ever let you go."

That did it. That started the tears. I quickly turned around in his arms and buried my head in his chest and cried. I wrapped my arms around his waist and held him so tight. I never wanted to let him go. I hated this so much. I know I am not a saint but why do I deserve this? He grabbed my arms to pull them away then reached down and lifted up my head so I was looking at him. "Babe, what's wrong? I thought we were having a good night."

I nodded, "It has been a great night that is the problem!" I yelled.

He looked confused, "I don't understand."

I pulled completely away from him, walking back a couple of steps but never taking my eyes off of his, "I hate this! I hate this stupid disease! I hate that there is nothing that doctors can do to save me! I hate that I don't have a lot of time left with you! I hate that for the first time in my life I have someone that actually loves me and I will only get to experience that for a few short months! I hate everything right now!"

I was screaming and probably had neighbors looking out their windows at me thinking I was insane, but I didn't care. I was so angry and I didn't know what else to do. Mason continued looking at me, letting me vent my frustrations. He wasn't saying anything at first so I figured I must have him second guessing spending this time with me until he finally said something, and what he did said almost knocked me to my knees. "Marry me."

What the fuck? "Mason, are you drunk again?" I asked completely serious. I am starting to wonder if it really was water he was drinking at the restaurant.

He smiled at me, "I am completely sober, babe, I promise," he lifted one eyebrow, "your driving helped me with that."

That made me giggle, "You cannot seriously want to marry me Mason. I am sick and I am dying."

He finally took a step towards me and grabbed both of my hands, "I have never been more serious about anything in my entire life. I promise you that. I don't care about you being sick. I just want to spend what time you do have left together, loving you, making you breakfast in bed, making love to you every day, seeing you sleeping next to me, all of it."

"You can do all of that anyway, Mason. I am your girlfriend, I am with you until the end."

"Well I don't want to do all of that with my girlfriend, I want to do all of that with my wife. The fact that you are dying doesn't make me love you any less. If anything it truly makes me realize how short life can be and I want to make sure that there are no regrets. I love you Scotti. You are my entire life and I want to marry you. If you don't feel comfortable with it, I completely understand. I won't pressure you into doing something you don't want to, but I have to be honest and let you know that I have been thinking about this since we were at the beach and even trying to talk myself out of it. Not because I don't want to marry you, but because we just met and I didn't want to scare you. Then I decided to see how tonight goes and maybe ask you tomorrow, but now, standing on this sidewalk, I couldn't wait anymore. I just don't want to waste any more time. We may not be able to change what is happening to you, but we can definitely dictate how our lives go until then."

I am listening to his speech, already knowing my answer, but not saying anything. I still feel angry but that anger has simmered down quite a bit. I squeezed his hands then take a deep breath and smile at him, "Honey, I love you so much. I would love nothing more than to marry you."

"Sooooo, is that a yes?" He asks me.

I nod my head, "That's not just a yes, that is a HELL YES!" I screamed.

Mason smiled widely then immediately picked me up and kissed me. I wrapped my legs around his waist and before I know it, he is sprinting down the street towards his house with me still in his arms. As soon as we get to his front door he reaches into his pocket to grab his keys, never letting me go, and unlocks the door. We get inside and he kicks the door closed. He takes me to his bedroom and gently laid me on the bed and stands up. "More than anything, I would love to make you my wife tonight but since that is not possible, I would love to make love to my fiancée, if you are ok with that."

I climb up until I am sitting on my knees directly in front of him, "I would more than love that." I tell him then gently kiss him on the lips.

We quickly get undressed. We make love with nothing but the light of the moon. We hold each other and make promises to one another. We fall asleep wrapped in each other's arms, feeling nothing but love.

Tomorrow we will wake up but instead of it being just a typical Thursday, we are going to become husband and wife, until death do us part.

Seventeen

Mason

I had a whole romantic proposal planned in my head but when we were standing on the street and the tears were running down Scotti's face, I knew I needed to do it right then and there. The look on her face was priceless. A mixture of shock and love. I didn't know if she would say yes but the relief I felt when she did was like nothing I have ever felt before.

When we woke up this morning I was so anxious and wanted nothing more than to rush to the courthouse, get our marriage license and get married. Scotti on the other hand was calm and cool. I made us breakfast and we sat together at the table, talking about the day like it wasn't the most important day of our lives. Something seemed off with her though and I was starting to think she was having second thoughts.

I reached over and laid my hand on top of hers, "Scotti, if this is too fast for you, I completely understand. I don't want you to do anything that makes you uncomfortable."

She shakes her head then looks down, "It's not that at all, I promise."

"What's wrong then? Would you rather do a big wedding? I can arrange that."

"I have no family or friends Mason. I am fine with our original plan. I want to become your wife today, I really do, more than anything, but I'm sick," she said with sadness.

I pull her hand to my lips and kiss it, "I know babe. But I want to marry you anyway, in sickness and in health."

"No, that's not what I mean," she says then sighs, "I mean I am sick today. I don't feel very well and this food is actually making me a bit nauseous."

Fuck, I haven't seen Scotti sick yet and certainly wasn't expecting it today, especially after the night we had last night. "Why don't we try this again tomorrow then? I don't want you to feel like shit on your wedding day."

"I just need to rest for a bit then I will be fine. Do you mind if I just go take a little nap? I should feel better after then we can go to the courthouse. I really want this to be our wedding day. I don't want to wait until tomorrow."

I take her hand and we both stand, "Of course not. Let me get you into bed. If you don't feel good after your nap, we will get married tomorrow. It's only one day, no big deal."

She stops walking then squeezes my hand, "It's a big deal to me. Today is the day. Just let me get a little rest and I will be good to go, I promise."

I was worried that she was going to push herself, even if she wasn't feeling completely good, but I wasn't about to tell her no. I may not have known her long but one thing I have learned is that there is no arguing with her when she has her mind set.

We walked hand in hand to the bedroom and she climbed into the bed and as soon as her head hit the pillow she was sound asleep. I covered her with a blanket then quietly walked out to the kitchen to get our breakfast mess cleaned up. This is the first taste of what's to come and I am already feeling incredible sadness. The next few months are going to be some of the hardest months, for both of us, but I also want to make sure I make her happier than she has ever been. Of all people in the world, Scotti deserves that.

Now

"Mr. Shaw?" I heard my name being called by a nurse and realized I had fallen asleep under this tree in front of the hospital. I immediately jump up.

"Is Scotti okay?" I ask in a panic.

"Yes Sir, she is fine, she is asking for you though."

I immediately start sprinting to Scotti's room. I wasn't planning on dozing off and I hate for Scotti to wake up without me being there. I don't ever want her to feel like she is alone. As I get to her room and walk in, I see her tiny body lying in bed and as soon as she hears me she slowly turns her head towards me and smiles. "Hey honey, where did you run off to?"

I sit down on the chair next to her bed and gently grab her hand and kiss it, "I'm so sorry babe. I went downstairs to sit under the big tree out front and ended up falling asleep."

"Don't be sorry. You obviously needed the sleep." Her voice was sounding weaker and weaker and with every word she spoke I could feel my heart splitting a little more.

"I just don't want you to ever think I left. I want to be here every time you wake from your nap." I explained to her.

"Mason…She was having a hard time breathing so I reached over for the oxygen mask that was next to her and put it on her face. It took her a few minutes but she was finally breathing better, not good, but better. I hate seeing her like this. Just having a short conversation takes everything out of her. I rub the top of her head to soothe her and once she feels her breathing is good she removes the mask from her face. "Mason, I could never think you left me but you need a break from all of this. It's okay. Really."

"Please don't say that Scotti. I don't want a break from this and I certainly don't need one. I just didn't sleep great last night. I feel better now though."

Truth be told, I did need a break from this. Not from Scotti, hell no. I need a break from all of the sadness and doctors and nurses and dying. My wife has changed so much in the months that I have known her. She is thin and brittle and can barely get a couple of sentences out without needing oxygen. She is sad and scared and hurting and angry and I can't do anything to make it better. I am furious inside and would commit murder if it meant fixing Scotti.

"I love you." She tells me in a weak voice.

I lean in and kiss her lips then sit down on the bed beside her. "Can I tell you a story?" I ask her.

She smiles, "Only if it is my most favorite story in the world."

I smile back at her, "It certainly is," I turn and adjust myself so I am lying right next to her. I carefully lift her head with one arm while I slide my other arm under her then lay her head down on my chest. "Are you comfortable?" I ask her.

"This is always my most comfortable spot." She says quietly.

I kiss the top of her head then lean back, "Okay. So, once upon a time, on a beautiful fall day, I married the most beautiful woman in the world…"

Eighteen

Scotti

I wake up and look over at the clock and realize I have been sleeping for four hours so I jump out of bed and immediately run to the living room, looking for Mason. As soon as I throw the door open I see Mason running towards me, "Scotti, are you okay?"

"Do we still have time? Did I sleep too long?" I wanted today to be our day, not tomorrow, not next week, today.

"Babe, it's only noon. We have plenty of time. But, first, how are you feeling?"

I felt relief, knowing we could still have get married today, "Much better. I needed that nap."

Mason smiled at me then wrapped his arms around me, "I still think we should wait until tomorrow, until you have a full day to just rest."

"NO!" I yell making Mason flinch, "I'm sorry, I just don't want to wait until tomorrow. Please, can we get married today?"

"Anything you want. Let's get dressed and get out of here."

We walked into the bedroom and Mason stops and turns to look at me, "I know you probably want a dress so we can stop somewhere and get whatever you want. It will be my wedding gift to you."

His thoughtfulness continuously makes me melt inside, but I didn't care about having a dress. "Unless you prefer me to wear a dress, I was actually thinking I could just wear the clothes I have. I am not typically a person to wear dresses but I don't want to embarrass you at all."

"Babe, you could never embarrass me. I just want you to be comfortable."

"This is comfortable to me." I said, smiling at him, while pointing at my jeans and shirt lying on his dresser.

"Okay, then it's perfect for me too."

We both decided we better shower before we leave and even though I felt better after my nap, I was still a little weak, so our joint shower was just that, a shower. I never thought washing each others' back could be so intimate but that shower was definitely one of the most romantic things I have ever experienced.

After getting dressed we jumped inside Mason's truck and drove down to the courthouse. Getting our license was a breeze, but we had about a two hour wait for the judge to marry us. Mason's leg was bouncing the entire time and I was getting worried. I reached over and put my hand on his leg, "Mason..."

He stopped me before I could say anymore, "Nope, don't say it. I am not having any doubts. I am just anxious. I want you to be my wife and I am just tired of waiting, that's all."

I smiled at him, not only because of what he said, but because of the fact that he knew what I was going to say to him before I even said it. That is usually something that happens when couples have been together for a long time but Mason can already read me like a book. I think that is true love.

I feel warm inside and even though I didn't doubt my decision before, I knew in that very moment that this is the best decision I have ever made. "Mason, can I tell you why I was so insistent on us getting married today?"

He stops bouncing his leg then looks over at me, "Of course. You can tell me anything."

I don't know how I managed to fill out my paperwork for our marriage license, sitting right next to him, and him not even see this. I wasn't hiding it on purpose; it just had not come up. I guess now is as good of time as any.

"Well, um, today is my birthday…"

"Wait what? Today is your birthday?" He says, cutting me off.

"Yes, but let me finish," he stops then lets me continue, "today is my birthday and in all of the years I have been on this Earth, I have never had a good birthday," I can feel a tear falling down my face and Mason reaches up and wipes it off then kisses me on the cheek. "And, well, I couldn't think of a better way to celebrate my last birthday that I will ever have, than by marrying you."

Mason takes in a deep breath and just when it looks like he is about to argue with me, he stops himself. There really isn't a reason to disagree since we both know there is no way I will survive six months, let alone another year. He stands up then walks over to the window and looks outside so I walk over to him and wrap my arms around him and lay my head on his back. "I'm sorry."

He turns around and pulls me against his chest, "Don't be sorry Scotti. I know we cannot control any of this but that doesn't make me feel okay about it. I just hate the thought of losing you."

"You won't ever lose me honey," I lay my hand on his chest, "I will always be in your heart and nothing will ever change that."

"Scottlyn and Mason?" We both turn and the judge is standing outside the door with a clipboard.

"Yes sir." Mason says, then grabs my hand and we walk over to him.

"Are you two ready to become husband and wife?" The judge asks with a smile.

"Yes, sir, more than ever." Mason tells him.

As soon as we walk inside, the judge walks up to his desk and we stand side by side in front of it. This is something I never imagined happening but today it really is, and I will always remember this day as the best day of my entire life.

Nineteen

Mason

"Do you, Mason, take Scottlyn, to be your wife? To have and to hold, for richer and for poorer, in sickness and in health, 'til death do you part?" This judge has absolutely no idea how much these vows represent us right now, not years down the road.

"I do." I say, with no hesitation, while staring into Scotti's eyes and smiling. She smiles back at me and I swear she is glowing.

"Do you, Scottlyn, take Mason to be your husband…"

"I DO!" She yells, making the judge and myself laugh. She looks over at the judge, "You don't need to finish. My answer is the same no matter what."

The judge nods his head and smiles, "Okay do you have rings?"

I shake my head, a little disappointed, "No, we are going to get those later."

I look back over at Scotti and instead of her being upset that she doesn't have a ring, she has the biggest smile I have ever seen on her face.

"Well, there is nothing more to say then, I now pronounce you husband and wife. Mason, you may kiss your wife."

And I do. I pull Scotti to me so fast she gasps then I plant my lips to hers in the best kiss I have ever shared with a woman in my entire life. She wraps her arms around my neck and kisses me back. We continue like that until we hear the judge clearing his throat. "Sorry," Scotti says, a little embarrassed as she pulls away from me.

He smiles at her, "No need to be. Congratulations to both of you." He shakes both of our hands, signs off on the marriage certificate and we are on our way.

I am kind of glad that our wedding was so delayed because it makes the timing of our next stop perfect. On our drive I can't help but constantly look over at Scotti and the smile that never leaves her face. She looks happy and content and I feel the same way.

As soon as we pull into the parking lot of our destination, Scotti perks up and smiles even wider, "Mason?"

I reach across the console and pull her to me, "I couldn't think of a better place to spend our wedding night then watching the sunset from the place that we first met."

She nods and even though she is trying really hard to hold them in, a couple tears fall, "I love you so much Mason Shaw. This is the happiest day of my whole life."

"I love you more Scottlyn Shaw. You are the best thing that has ever happened to me." I kiss her then jump out of the truck and run to her side and open the door. Before she even gets a chance to get out I reach in and pick her up.

"What are you doing? You are supposed to carry me over the threshold, not the beach," She says laughing.

"I can do both. Just having you in my arms is what I want right now."

I carry her towards the sand and get to "our spot" and sit down, holding her in my lap. "This is so perfect Mason, thank you," she says as she lays her head back against my chest.

I hold her tighter then kiss her on the side of her face, "I know we don't have a lot of days left, but the ones we do have I will make sure are the most perfect days of your life."

She sits up, then turns so she is straddling me and puts both her hands on either side of my face, "Honey, if I were to die tomorrow, I would die the happiest woman to ever walk the planet, and that is one hundred percent because of you. Thank you for not only making me your wife but loving me like nobody else ever has."

"I will never stop loving you Scotti, never." I tell her honestly because even though we won't have a long life together, nothing and nobody will ever get me to stop loving her. "Happy Birthday, Baby," I tell her then gently kiss her soft lips. She smiles then turns back around just as the sun is setting.

I know my love for this woman is something I will never have with anyone else and even with our lives together being short lived, I know I just made the best decision I ever have made by marrying her and for as long as I live, there will never be one ounce of regret.

Twenty

Scotti

My favorite and most relaxing thing in the world is the beach at sunset. After Charlie died and I started living in the women's shelter, I would take long walks and just think. One day I walked to the beach right before sunset and stared out into the ocean. As the sun was setting I realized I was more relaxed than I had ever been, so I started coming here every evening.

For the week that Mason and I were apart, I missed a sunset every single one of those nights. My perfect place reminded me of Mason, and as much as I really liked him, I was afraid of running into him. I missed the sunsets so much though. It may seem like no big deal to some people but when you have absolutely nothing in your life, you look forward to those little things that bring you happiness and peace. I was told one day, not too long ago, that my cancer had spread and there was nothing more the doctors could do to save me. I could do chemo but it would only prolong my life, not save me. That day, I walked down to the beach and cried for hours. I asked God why this had to happen to me. I asked God to let my death be peaceful and painless. I asked God if it was possible for me to die happy. I knew that last request was a long shot but that very same day, as I sat staring into the water while saying my prayers, my knight and shining armor appeared. He comforted me, a stranger, instead of walking right past me like everyone else did. He cared for me right away. He fell in love with me almost immediately. Best of all, he made me happy.

I asked for happiness in the end and I got it. Mason is everything I could possibly want in a man. I know, even if I wasn't down on that beach that day that we would have somehow found each other. We were meant to be together. I hate that I have pulled him into my nightmare, but whenever I express those feelings to him I can see that he gets upset. This isn't ideal for either of us but it's the way it is so it is up to us to make the best of it.

I am lost in thought when I am startled by my body leaving the ground, "Mason, what are you doing?" I ask him as he is picking me up off the sand.

"I am taking you to our home. I need to make love to my wife." Chills immediately covered my body. I am a wife. I have a husband and not just any husband, I have the most amazing husband that has ever existed. I am the luckiest woman alive.

"Yes, please," is all I could say before Mason starts sprinting to the truck. My body is bouncing all over the place, making me laugh. I have never laughed so much in my life until I met him.

We get to the truck and he is completely out of breath but still holding me in his arms. I start squirming but instead of him putting me down, he just holds me tighter. "Just give me a minute, I will be fine." Mason says between breaths.

"Honey, you will recover a lot faster if you put me down." I tell him, although I do love the feeling of being in his arms.

He grabs his keys from his pocket, clicks the key FOB to unlock the door and opens it, without me even slipping a little. "Baby, if I could hold you every single day and never put you down, I would." He kisses me then gently puts me inside. After closing the door and running around the front of the truck he quickly jumps inside and starts the engine. "Are you okay with heading home or is there something else you would like to do first.

I shake my head and smile, maybe a little too excitedly, knowing that getting home means naked time with my sexy husband. Mason laughs and before I know it he is peeling out of the parking lot. He reaches over and holds my hand as he maneuvers through traffic. No words are spoken, none needed to be. Tonight is our wedding night and I know Mason will make it special. Tonight there is no cancer, no dying and no end. Tonight it is just us.

Twenty One

Mason

Now

"That was my favorite memory. The best day of my entire life," Scotti says quietly, trying to hide the fact that she has been crying during my story. I wrap my arms around her tighter and just let her cry. After a couple of minutes, she gives up hiding it and makes it known. "Why is this happening to me, Mason?"

I sigh, wishing I had wise words to say to make her feel better, "I don't know baby, I wish I did."

We lay silent like that, her head on my chest and my arms wrapped around her, for so long, that I think she has fallen asleep until she slowly lifts her head and looks at me with her red eyes, "Can I tell you something?"

I smile at her, "You know you can tell me anything."

She smiles back at me, "Even though we didn't get a lot of time together, meeting you and marrying you was the best thing to ever happen to me. I want to apologize to you, for putting you through all of this…"

"Scotti!"

She put her hand up to stop me from saying any more, "Please let me finish. As I was saying, I *want* to apologize, but I won't. Lately I have been trying to put myself in your shoes. Trying to think about how I would feel if the tables were turned and you were the one lying here dying." She stops a minute to catch her breath. "What I have concluded is that I wouldn't regret our time together one bit. I would rather have you for that short period of time than to have never met you. I was never truly happy until I met you. I never experienced love until I met you." She stopped again, reaching over and placing the oxygen mask on her face. After a short time she pulled it away and continued, "I know you feel the same way that I do so I will not apologize, instead I will envy you. Yes, you will lose me but you also get to remember us. You get to look at pictures of us. You get to look at the silly cards we got for each other. I can't take any of that with me when I go so all I can hope for is that heaven allows me to remember you and our memories too. If that is the case then it truly will be heaven."

I am not sure what to say so I say the most honest thing that I am thinking, "I am not sure if having all of that is good or bad," I am ashamed but it is truly how I am feeling. How can it be a good thing to be stuck on this Earth without the love of your life and all you have to remember her by is pictures and fucking cards? That does not sound great to me at all.

Scotti grabs my hand, pulls it to her lips and gently kisses it, "I don't know either. I don't know if those things would make me feel good or bad but sitting where I am right now, it seems like a good thing. Where I am going is a place that I have to go to without you. If you can't keep me physically alive then the next best thing is to keep my memory alive." She pauses to take another deep breath. All of this talking is wearing her down but I know my wife, she will stop when she wants, not when I say. "Honey, I just don't want you to give up living because I no longer am. I want you to experience life and I really want you to experience love again. You deserve that."

The last time we had this discussion it ended in a huge fight so this is not a conversation I want to have again. How can I possibly love like this again? I never loved until Scotti. I never want to love anyone ever again. Scotti, and only Scotti, will always have my heart.

I adjust her body so I can slide off the bed without hurting her, then I walk over to the window and look into the empty sky.

"Mason?"

"Stop Scotti. Please. I cannot talk about this anymore." I am trying to keep the anger out of my voice but I don't think I am doing a very good job.

"Mason, please don't be upset with me," She says sadly.

I turn around and walk back over to her bed, "I am trying not to be, I really am. I think I am more pissed about the situation than I am with what you said."

She reaches for my hand and squeezes it weakly, "If the tables were turned, you would want the same for me. Just think about that."

Sadly, with the way I feel now, I would not feel the same. The thought of her with anyone else puts an anger in me that I don't like. She lays her head down, pulls my hand to her lips and kisses it, then closes her eyes. She is exhausted and needs to rest. This is the most she has talked at one time in a couple of weeks. I lean down, kiss her lips then her forehead and sit down on the chair next to her bed. She still has a hold of my hand, and I don't want her to let it go. I love the feeling of her hand in mine. I lay my head back and start to close my eyes, needing some more rest. When the time comes, and she no longer has another breath inside of her little body, I don't know how I will ever be able to let her go and walk away for good.

Then

I am pretty sure I am currently having the best dream of my life. I am soaked in sweat, can hardly catch my breath and when I turn my head, I see the most beautiful woman in the world lying next to me, completely naked, and covered in sweat herself. I can't take my eyes off of her. Not only did I just have the most amazing sexual experience of my life, but I had it with my wife! I don't know what I did to get so lucky but I will be forever thankful for whatever it is.

"Why are you staring at me?" Scotti asks me with a giggle.

"I just can't believe that you're my wife," I roll towards her and cup her cheek, "you are so fucking beautiful. I love you so much."

She smiles, that billion dollar smile, then leans towards me and kisses me, "I love you, Mason."

I kiss her back then pull her entire body up against mine. I just can't touch her enough. "Are you cold? Do you need a blanket?" I ask her.

"No, I'm okay, but there is something I do need." She says quietly, almost too quiet.

She raises her head but she is not looking me in the eyes, "Anything, baby."

She lets out a long breath, bites her lip then smiles, "Um, well, can we do that again?"

I almost laugh at how adorably shy she is being, but catch myself, not wanting to embarrass her. "We can do that as much as you like. I will never say no to you. To be honest, I don't think I could say no if I wanted to."

I roll her over then cover her body with my own. I am not even inside of her and the intimacy of this moment is incredible. I kiss her mouth, then her chin and slowly move down to her breasts. As soon as I have one of her nipples in my mouth a moan comes out of her. I gently suck on her breast, then the other one and make my way back up to her mouth, "I love you, Scotti."

"I love you, Mason," she tells me as I slowly push inside of her. As soon as I am completely in I start moving slowly, kissing her and repeating over and over how much I love her.

"Mason, stop." She says abruptly.

"Oh God, baby, did I hurt you?" I am still inside of her but not moving a muscle.

She nods her head, "No, I didn't mean that, sorry. I just… I mean, I absolutely love making love to you. I love it all and please don't take this the wrong way but right now, I don't want to make love. Right now, I would love nothing more than for you fuck me stupid."

My wife is a fucking goddess! She talks sweet, she looks sweet but damn she has a mouth on her!

She gives me her innocent smile, making me chuckle, but I can't wait any longer so I start moving inside of her, quickly picking up the pace. I let go of her hands to lift her hips and when I do she takes her fingernails and scratches them down my back. Fuck this feels incredible.

The sweat was building up between us, a lot more than before, and I felt like I could go on like this forever. "Mason, harder, please. Don't stop!" She yells, between breaths.

I sat up on my knees, never pulling out of her, and lifted her legs so her ankles were resting on my shoulders, and continued pumping inside of her. That caused a lot more than moans to come out of her mouth. "Holy shit, Mason!" Scotti screamed and I continued at my pace.

I knew I wasn't going to last much longer but I needed Scotti to come before me so I increased the pace. That's all it took. Seconds later Scotti let out a scream so loud, I was pretty sure I was going to be partially deaf from it. I continued until I felt that build up then came with such force that I thought I was going to pass out from the pleasure.

I slowed down my pace until I couldn't move anymore, gently took her legs off my shoulders then collapsed my body on top of hers. We were both breathing heavily and slick with sweat and when I lifted my head and looked into Scotti's eyes, I knew she was more than satisfied, as was I.

I gently kissed her lips then laid my head on her chest. She wrapped her arms around me and kissed the top of my head. "I love you Mason. I will never stop loving you. Until the day I die, you will always be my everything."

I closed my eyes, feeling exactly the same way, but knowing that she will never have the ultimate pain of missing me like I will be missing her. I whispered to her that I loved her and let the tears fall, knowing that time was coming sooner than either of us would ever want.

Twenty Two

Scotti

I stretch my body and can hear it creaking like I am an eighty year old woman. Last night was so hot and I couldn't get enough of my new husband. After our hotter than hell sex, we held each other for quite some time until I got the urge to go at it again. I could tell Mason was more than happy to just roll over and go to sleep but he never denied me and we made love until the early morning hours.

Mason is still sleeping next to me so I slowly crawl out of bed and head into the bathroom to get cleaned up. I know if I turn on the shower, he will wake up, so I brush my teeth and hair, throw on some sweats of his that are lying in the floor, and quietly exit the bathroom then tip toe out of the bedroom to go make some breakfast. I am starving and I know Mason will be too once he gets up. I will now begin my wifely domestic duties. I love the sound of that.

When I get into the kitchen I stop and look around, not knowing where anything is at. The last time I tried to cook Mason breakfast I got as far as finding a bowl to mix eggs then was interrupted with hot sex. Mason and I have moved at such a fast pace that I don't even know where to find a pan to cook in. My happy high is suddenly gone and I am now feeling like I don't belong. I drop to the floor on my knees and start to silently cry. I cry and cry and cry some more until I feel my husband's arms wrapping around my body. He doesn't speak and ask me if I am okay, which I appreciate. I think he realizes that I am overwhelmed. I don't know how he does it but he seems to know exactly how I am feeling all the time.

He lets me finish crying and when I am done, I turn my body around to face him and as soon as I look into his sleep deprived eyes, my world is suddenly all better. I wipe the tears off my face then kiss his cheek, "I'm sorry, I couldn't find a pan." I tell him, realizing how ridiculous that sounds.

"Don't be sorry Scotti, you needed to get it out. Next time though, don't do it alone. I am your husband and I am here for you through everything and I can help you find a pan."

It is then, that I realize, this wasn't about a pan at all and suddenly I am angry. I jump up, grab the first thing that I manage to get my hands on, which happens to be a glass, and throw it against the wall, shattering it and making Mason jump. "Scotti, what the hell was that for?"

"Why? Why do you have to be so wonderful? Why do you always have to say the most perfect things to me? What in the fuck did I do to deserve this hell?" I am screaming, not thinking about what I am saying but just spitting it out.

"Hell? Being with me is hell?" Now Mason is yelling but I think his yelling is more out of hurt than anger.

"YES!" I scream off the top of my lungs. Now the tears are pouring down my face so I take a deep breath and speak more calmly, "It's hell because it doesn't get to last until we are old like most married couples do. It's hell because we won't get too many nights like last night. It's hell because I won't even be alive long enough to figure out where the fucking pans are kept!"

My heart hurt. It might have seemed stupid to care about something like a pan, but at that time it seemed valid to me. I dropped my head in shame and it only took all of about a second for Mason to get to me and pull me into his arms. "I don't know the right words to say to you. The only thing I can say is that we just need to live for today. Then tomorrow when we wake up we will live for then. And so on and so on. That's the best thing we can do. We love each other too much to live the rest of the time we have together, no matter how short or long that will be, screaming in the middle of the kitchen. It's just not worth it."

What if tomorrow was the day that I was going to die and the last memory he had was me breaking a glass and having a meltdown. I nodded my head, agreeing with him. "You're right, I'm sorry Mason, I will try not to let these little things get to me."

He smiled at me then pulled me in to a tight hug. We held each other like that for a long time, until I felt him lifting me up and cradling me in his arms. I kissed him and then he gently set me down on top of the counter. "I need to get this glass cleaned up and I don't want you to get cut. Will you sit there until I am done?"

"I should be the one cleaning it up, I broke it." I moved like I was going to jump off the counter but Mason held me, stopping me.

"Stay put. I will take care of it." He walked over to the refrigerator, grabbed a bottle of water out then handed it to me. "Here, I am sure all of that crying made you thirsty. Let me get this cleaned up, then we will go take a shower together, get dressed and go out for breakfast."

"Okay." I said quietly. Mason went out to the garage and grabbed a broom and dustpan and got to work cleaning up the glass.

"Hey, Mason?"

"Yeah, baby?"

"Do you realize I just went a little crazy over a pan?"

He nodded, "Yeah, baby… I do."

He didn't even crack a smile when he answered me and that made me start laughing. I laughed so hard that he started laughing then I even snorted from laughing so hard making him laugh harder. After that bit of drama, we both needed this release. I know there is absolutely nothing that can be done to save me so instead of living day to day feeling sorry for myself, I am just going to live. I am going to make sure Mason knows every single day how much I love him and I am going to make sure that when I am gone, Mason has nothing but happy memories of our time together. That is the only gift I can possibly give him from here on out.

Twenty Three

Mason

Seeing Scotti upset and angry in the middle of our kitchen just about broke me. With the exception of the night I asked her to marry me, she has been pretty strong about everything, shedding a couple of tears here and there, but nothing like this morning. Although what I told her was the absolute truth, that we need to live each day like it is the last, it was hard for me to even say those words.

After our shower, we both got dressed and headed downtown to get some breakfast then walk around the little shops. We decided to have a stress free and do nothing but window shop kind of day. I pulled into the parking lot of a small café that I have been to, many times before and before I can get out and open Scotti's door for her, she is out and heading towards the door of the restaurant.

"Scotti, wait up." I said as I am running towards her.

She stopped then turned and laughed, "I'm sorry, this place is so cute. I got a little excited."

I smiled at her, grabbed her hand then started walking towards the entrance, "You have never been here before?"

She shook her head, "Nope, never popped that cherry. I am a café virgin."

I started laughing, happy that she is happy again, "Okay. Well then I am honored to be the one that gets to pop that cherry."

That made her giggle, "Honey, in the last few weeks you have popped every single cherry there is to pop."

All of this cherry popping talk was causing feelings inside that we needed to stop immediately because all I could think about was lifting that skirt that Scotti was wearing and fucking her right in the middle of this parking lot. I really didn't feel like going to jail so I quickly had to start thinking of something else to get rid of those thoughts.

We got inside and seated, looked over our menus then placed our orders with the waitress. Scotti took a sip of her water then looked over at me, "Mason, will you tell me about your Aunt and Uncle that raised you?"

It wasn't something I have ever talked about to anyone, but Scotti is my wife and I wanted her to know everything about me, "Of course. Well, my Aunt Rose was my Mom's sister. After my parents were killed she took me in with no hesitation. My Uncle Dale was a little hesitant at first, but he quickly warmed up to the idea. Everything was going okay until I started high school. That's when I turned into a teenage prick."

Scotti's eyes went wide, probably surprised by how outspoken I was, but I was not going to blame anything on my Aunt and Uncle. Everything that happened with them was all because of me.

"I started drinking with friends, if that's what you want to call them. I snuck out or sometimes didn't come home all night. My Aunt would report me missing, cops would find me, I would get grounded, but that didn't stop me. Whatever they told me to do, I did exactly the opposite. I made their lives a living hell. I was angry about losing my parents, but Rose and Dale didn't deserve the hell I put them through. The day I turned 18 they kicked me out. I could see how much it hurt Rose to do that, but she needed to do what was necessary to save her marriage. I was definitely creating a rift between the two of them."

"When was the last time you spoke to them?" She asked me.

I took a deep breath, ashamed in myself, "The day they told me to leave. Rose took me aside alone, told me to get my shit together, and then I could come back. I know Dale would never agree to that so even after I got sober, I never tried to get their help. I worked shitty jobs, slept on some couches, but I never went back to them again."

The waitress walked over at that moment and put our plates of food in front of us. Scotti started digging into her pancakes as I was scarfing down my eggs like it was my first meal of the week. With the exception of our forks hitting our plates, there was silence.

"Mason?" Scotti said, after a few minutes of eating.

"Yes, baby."

"I want us to go see your Aunt and Uncle." I dropped my fork and just stared at her, hoping that she was just giving me shit.

Once I realized she was serious I shook my head, "Absolutely not." I picked my fork back up and continued eating. I heard Scotti sigh, but I didn't look back at her again until I heard her fork hit her plate.

When I looked up she was glaring at me, "What?" I asked her.

"Don't 'what' me, Mason Shaw. We are going to see your Aunt and Uncle and you are going to make things right with them. You all deserve that."

"Scotti, I said no, now drop it. They don't want anything to do with me and I don't blame them one bit."

"Mason, you are their family. They love you. If they didn't your Aunt wouldn't have offered you to go back once you straightened up. Stop being so stubborn and just go see them."

By this time, I had lost my appetite. Sure, over the years I had thought about going to see them but I quickly talked myself out of it. I ran my hands up and down my face and when I pulled them away, Scotti was still staring at me. "Why are you so determined to get my relationship with them back?"

She folded her hands in front and gave me a completely serious expression, "Because Mason, after I am gone, you are going to need people to lean on."

My heart dropped. "I won't need anyone, Scotti. Can we please drop this subject?"

She shook her head, "No."

I definitely married the most stubborn woman on the planet, "Scotti, I don't want to talk about you dying anymore. Remember, we are living each day."

"Mason, I told you I would live each day without feeling sorry for myself. I didn't say we would never talk about it. We have to talk about it. It's our life whether we like it or not." She took a deep breath and continued, "you not only need to go make amends with your Aunt and Uncle for the past, but I bet it would make them so happy to know how great you have turned out."

I sat thinking about what she was saying, knowing she was right but not wanting to admit it.

"Besides," she continued, "I bet they would love to meet your amazingly brilliant and wonderful wife. I mean, seriously Mason, how could they not?"

No matter what the circumstances are, Scotti could always put a smile on my face. "Don't forget beautiful," I tell her, then lean across the table and pull her to me so I could kiss her, "You're right, how could they not?"

"So then we can go?" I nodded to her and she smiled then kissed me and leaned back into her chair. She continued eating and all I could do was stare at her. She truly was so amazing and I couldn't believe how much I had fallen in love with her in just a short amount of time.

"So, when do you think we should do this, oh brilliant wife of mine?"

She laughed as I took a sip of water, "Right now."

I started choking, "WHAT?"

"Mason, do you have any other plans today?" She asked me.

"I thought we were going to spend the day downtown looking through all the shops together. I mean we are technically on our honeymoon."

"Well, things change. Finish your breakfast and let's get out of here. I am so excited." She clapped her hands and smiled but I could not join in on her excitement. My heart was racing and I could feel myself starting to sweat. I knew there would be a day when I would finally have to face my family but when I woke up this morning I certainly didn't think it was going to be today. I laid some money on the table then stood up and held my hand out for Scotti. We walked out towards the car, but before we got there she stopped and grabbed both of my hands.

"Mason, I know this is going to be hard for you but just remember, I am right by your side. For the rest of your life I will always be right by your side. Maybe not physically, but I will be here. And the two of us together can do anything."

I won't even argue with her on that. No matter what, she will always be with me, until the day I die.

Twenty Four

Mason

We have been sitting in my truck, across the street from my Aunt and Uncle's house for a good half hour or so. I have given Scotti at least a dozen excuses why we should just leave, but she won't have any of it. I have never in my life listened to other people and let them dictate what I do, however, this woman could tell me to chop off my right nut and I would probably do it just because she said so.

"Baby, I have been thinking…"

Scotti cuts me off before I can get another word out. "Nope, not another excuse, Mason. I understand needing to take some time, but you need to do this. I see how sad you are when you talk about them. I don't know what will happen today, but no matter what you can at least leave here knowing you at least tried. I promise you that a huge weight will be lifted from your shoulders."

Scotti is right as usual. I do feel sad when I think about everything I put them through and I do feel sad when I think about how it's been more than ten years since I have spoken a word to either of them. I pull her hand to my mouth, give it a small kiss then open the door and climb out of the truck. Scotti jumps out of the truck and runs to me then grabs my hand and smiles, silently letting me know she is here for me.

We walk hand in hand up the walk to the door. I slowly bring my hand up to the doorbell. I look over at Scotti before I ring it, "Well, here goes nothing."

My shaky finger pushes the doorbell and within a couple of seconds the door is opening and as soon as I lock eyes with her I feel like my legs are going to give out. "Mason?" Rose says in surprise.

"Hi, Aunt Rose." Just as I get her name out she immediately pulls me into a hug while she is sobbing loudly. I wrap my arms around her, having a hard time holding it together myself, and held her for several minutes. I didn't realize until this very moment exactly how much I really needed to do this. Rose's sobbing slows and as much as neither one of us wants to, we pull away from each other. She wipes her eyes and I look over at Scotti to see her reaction and she is also wiping the tears from her face.

"I think about you every day and hope and pray that you are okay. I can't believe you are actually standing here in front of me." She said with excitement while looking me over from head to toe.

"I'm sorry it took me so long to come back," I pull Scotti to my side, "Aunt Rose, this is my wife, Scotti. You can actually thank her for us coming here today."

Scotti reaches out to shake her hand but instead Rose pulls her into a hug. "You must be the reason my Mason looks so great," Rose says.

Scotti lets out an uncomfortable laugh, "It's so nice to meet you, ma'am." She says as they pull away from each other.

"Please sweetie, call me Rose, or Aunt Rose. I haven't heard that in so long, it sounds so great!"

"Then Aunt Rose it is." Scotti says with a smile.

Rose looked over at me, "You have got yourself a beautiful woman here, Mason."

"You don't have to tell me twice." I said with a smile, then leaned in and kissed Scotti's cheek.

"Are you able to stay a while? I would love to visit with you, Mason, and get to know Scotti." Scotti and I look over at each other, smile, and then nod our heads.

She turns to walk inside and we both follow. As soon as we get through the door I stop and take a look around. Not much has changed. Rose has the same furniture, same curtains, and same carpet. I look over to the mantle and there are still the same pictures of her and Uncle Dale… and one of the three of us. I don't even remember taking that picture, but I couldn't have been more than fourteen or so. I walk over and pick it up to look at it more closely.

"That is my favorite picture," Rose says from behind me, "my biggest regret is not taking more pictures of you," I turn to her and she places her hand on my cheek, "I have missed you so much."

"I missed you too Aunt Rose," I set the picture back on the mantle, and then turn back to her, "Where is Uncle Dale? I would love to see him too.

Rose gives me a small smile then grabs my hand and holds it in hers, "Sweetie, Uncle Dale passed away a little over two years ago."

I pull my hand away from hers and fall to my knees on the floor then drop my head, feeling lightheaded and sick to my stomach. No tears are falling. All I can think is that this is punishment for the way I acted. Scotti is immediately by my side with her arms around me and kissing the side of my face telling me she is sorry. I look up and notice Rose is sitting on the floor right in front of me. "I never got to apologize for the way I treated him," I tell her, "I never got to make amends with him. I never got to tell him how thankful I was for everything he did for me."

"Mason, sweetie, he knew. He loved you and he knew you loved him back. He also knew that you had been through hell losing your parents the way you did so he never harbored any bad feelings towards you at all. There were a couple of times we had talked about looking for you, to make sure you were okay, but we both knew that you would come home, once the time was right. It's okay that it wasn't right while he was still here, but he knows, Mason, he really does know."

I take a deep breath and look over at Scotti while still addressing Rose, "Do you believe our loved ones watch over us when we die, Aunt Rose?" Tears form in Scotti's eyes and she smiles at me.

"I have no doubt in my mind that they do. Losing Dale has been so hard. I spent many wonderful years with him, but I find great comfort in knowing that he is still here with me spiritually. I don't think I could have gotten through the past couple of years without that." There is sadness in

Rose's voice but she still has a slight smile on her face. I lean in and kiss Scotti, then reach out for Rose and hug her tight. My only thought right now is how right I hope she is, because I don't know how I will survive without Scotti once she is gone.

Twenty Five

Scotti

I hope more than anything, that the answer Rose gave to Mason about our loved ones after they die was comforting to him because it was certainly comforting to me. I never really thought about death until I got my cancer diagnosis and even then, it wasn't something I kept on my mind a lot. It wasn't until a month ago, when I met Mason and I finally had someone in my life that I loved, that I started thinking about what happens after a person dies. Rose seems convinced that Dale still watches over her. I hope that is the case because I can't imagine not seeing Mason, but there is a down side to that too. Do I want to see Mason sad all the time when I am gone? Do I want to see him move on with another woman? Kiss her, make love to her, marry her, have children with her? Yes, I want more than anything for him to be able to find someone and fall in love again, I just don't know if I want to be there to witness it.

"Baby, are you okay?" Mason asks, pulling me from my thoughts.

I nod to him, "Yes, of course, just thinking."

He nods and gives me a look, telling me he knows what I am thinking about, but doesn't say anything. We talk some more about Uncle Dale, learning that his death was a result of a massive heart attack that he had unexpectedly while working outside in the yard. I can't imagine waking up one day and out of the blue, losing your loved one so quickly like that. At least with my cancer, my death won't come out of nowhere with no time to prepare.

"Aunt Rose, can we treat you to dinner tonight? There are some great little restaurants around here," Mason asks her.

"I actually was just preparing a chicken before you got here, but I would love it if you both would stay and have dinner with me. That's a lot of food for just little old me." Rose says with a smile.

Mason turns to me and I nod then he turns back to Rose, "We would love to stay. Thank you."

She walks up to him and puts both hands on each side of his face, "My sweet Mason Shaw. You have grown up to be not only handsome but incredibly sweet and polite, just like your Mom."

He smiles at her, "My Mom wasn't the only influence I had Aunt Rose."

She tears up and nods her head then kisses Mason's cheek and walks into the kitchen.

"Is there anything I can do to help Aunt Rose," I ask her.

"Sure sweetie. I was going to make a salad. Would you mind getting everything cut up for that?"

"I would love to." Rose hands me a cutting board and knife, then gets everything for the salad out of the refrigerator and sets it on the counter next to me.

Mason sits on the chair at the counter across from me and smiles so I give him a wink. This has turned out so much better than I ever anticipated and all I want to do now is get Mason home and tear of his clothes. As if he knows exactly what I am thinking, he lifts one eyebrow at me then shakes his head while smiling. Yeah, he knows.

"So, why don't you two tell me all about how you met and your wedding, I have missed so much." Rose says, pulling us both out of our naughty thoughts.

Mason wasn't saying anything so I start, "Well, we actually met on the beach. Mason was out running and I was sitting on the sand watching the sunset. We started talking and instantly felt a connection to each other."

Mason continues, "Then I acted like a total asshat and let her leave and I never thought I would see her again. But I tracked her down, took her out on a date and fell in love with her immediately." He smiled at me and my insides were melting. Mason has always been romantic with me and we definitely fell in love fast, but hearing him saying that still gives me butterflies.

"It sounds like you both love each other very much. How long have you been married?" We both look at each other, then at Rose, and start laughing. "What is so funny?" She asks.

"Well," Mason says, "we have only been married a little over 24 hours."

Rose stops what she is doing and just stares at both of us with her mouth open, "You just got married yesterday?" She asks in shock.

We both nod then laugh again.

"Well, what the hell are you doing here then? You should be out, spending time with each other, not this old lady."

I finally pry my eyes away from my husband then look over at Rose, "This was actually my idea. Mason has talked about you and I could see how much he missed you. I didn't want to waste another day of him missing you so I suggested that we come see you, in hopes that when…" I stumbled over my words, almost saying too much, "I mean, I want him to be able to have a relationship with you so you both can be there for each other." I was making no sense at all and when I looked at Mason, his eyes were wide.

Rose was looking back and forth between us, suspiciously. She still had her knife in her hand then pointed it towards me, "What just happened there?"

I swallowed, "What do you mean?"

"I may not be a Mom, but I was like a Mom for many years and I can still detect when someone is not telling me something. You almost said something then stopped yourself. What is going on?"

Fuck. I had every intention on telling Rose but didn't want it to be on our very first visit with her.

"Aunt Rose, nothing is going on. Scotti is still just a little nervous about meeting you." I appreciated Mason trying to help, but I knew it wasn't going to work.

I let out a sigh then gently laid my knife on the cutting board and walked over to Mason. "I think we need to just tell her." Mason just nodded then we both looked at Rose. I took a deep breath and let it out slowly. "Rose, I love Mason, like I have never loved another person in my entire life. Mason and I met… just a few weeks ago."

Rose smiled like that bit of news didn't bother her a bit, "Sweetie, when you know you know. I think that's beautiful. I can tell that you are both incredibly in love with each other. You don't need to date for years to figure that out." She started to tear up which was making me do the same, "you stay true to each other and continue to love each other, then this is going to last until you are both old and wrinkly, like Dale and me."

I looked down when I felt the first tear fall, "That won't be happening with us Aunt Rose."

She looked at me confused. I think both by my statement and the fact that I was crying, "Why won't that be happening?"

I grab Mason's hand and he reaches up with his free one and wipes the tears. I stare into his eyes, not wanting to look away, "I don't have a choice," I look over at Rose, "I have cancer and I don't have very long to live."

Twenty Six

Mason

I hear a gasp out of Aunt Rose as soon as Scotti tells her she is dying, "But, you look perfectly healthy," She tells her.

Scotti smiles at her, "For the most part, I feel okay right now. I get tired a bit easier than I used to but I am still able to do everything I did before, just a little slower."

"There is nothing the doctors can do to heal you?" That's the same question I have asked a million times. The answer I get is never the one I want to hear.

"Unfortunately, no, the cancer has spread. I had originally decided to do chemo but it wasn't going to save me so the day I was supposed to start it, I changed my mind. I decided that, even if I don't live as long, at least I will live and not be as sick as I would have been with having chemo."

Rose isn't saying anything and I give Scotti and squeeze, reassuring her that everything is okay. "Aunt Rose, I found out the day I met her that she had cancer. I didn't know the extent of her illness but I did know. I married her, knowing that we would never celebrate our one year anniversary or grow old together but that didn't matter. I knew I loved her, that I am in love with her, and even with all of this, I couldn't imagine not having her in my life, no matter how short of time that is."

Rose has tears falling down her face so I let go of Scotti's hand and walk around the counter and pull her into a hug, "It's just not fair, Mason. I'm sorry. I shouldn't be crying when you both are going through all of this."

"It's okay," I tell her, "we have both done our share of crying and you are right, it's absolutely not fair at all. The only thing we can do now is make the most of the time we do have together."

She looks up at me, eyes still filled with tears, "Mason, you are an amazing young man. Most men would have run the other way and never looked back but you," she looks over at Scotti, "is he your only family dear?"

Scotti nods as a couple more tears fall.

Rose walks away from me and over to Scotti, "Not any more. I won't pretend to know what you are going through but I can tell you that you will never do it alone. You not only have Mason but you have me too. I hope that is okay with you."

Scotti drops her face into her hands and starts crying and Rose wraps her arms around her. I walk over and put my arms around both of them and I, myself, let a few tears flow right along with them.

We all got done with the crying, finish preparing and cooking dinner and for the first time in years I sat down at Aunt Rose's table and ate a meal. Having this amazing woman who was like a Mom to me on one side and my incredible wife on the other side, made me realize just how truly blessed I am.

We finished eating and got everything cleaned up then started saying our goodbyes to Rose, "We would love to have you over for dinner one night soon Aunt Rose." Scotti told her as we were heading to the door.

"I would love that dear. I am retired now so any night is really okay for me."

I looked over at Scotti then back to Rose, "Well, we are going to take a few days, to have some sort of honeymoon, so can you come over Thursday evening?"

Rose nodded, "I would love that."

We exchanged phone numbers and I texted Rose our address and directions to get there. We hugged and said our goodbyes then Scotti and I walked out and got inside my truck.

I had both my hands on the steering wheel but wasn't moving. Scotti laid one of her hands on top of mine, "Honey, today was a great day. Are you happy?"

I slowly looked over at her and smiled, "You know what? I am so happy. I didn't know how it would go, but I am so glad I listened to you and did this. It really did lift a heavy weight off my shoulders."

I pulled her to me and gave her a slow kiss but not being alone with her all day finally hit me and our slow kiss turned into a heated kiss. She opened her mouth slightly, allowing my tongue to slide right in. She reached up and grabbed my hair and pulled me closer to her and next thing I know she was climbing on to my lap.

"Baby, we have to stop," I tell her while panting.

Scotti wasn't having any part of that. She pulled me back to her and had her tongue in my mouth before I could even think.

I gently pushed her back, "Scotti, if we could, I would be stripping you naked and fucking you right here in this truck, I just don't think my Aunt would enjoy that show too much."

Scotti eyes got wide like she just realized what we were doing, "Shit, Mason, I just tried to have sex with you right in front of your Aunt's house! " She put her hands over her face and shook her head.

I pulled her hands away from her face then smiled at her, loving the fact that she is feeling that strong need for me just as I am for her, "Baby, don't be embarrassed. We both got a little carried away. Right now, I would love more than anything to take you home and christen every single inch of that house before we finally fall asleep, if that is okay with you of course."

Scotti smiled then jumped back over to her seat and quickly put her seat belt on. I was watching her and smiling when she looked back over at me,

"What the hell are you waiting for? We have some christening to do. DRIVE!"

I laughed then put the truck in gear and headed out. We couldn't go anywhere too far for an exotic honeymoon with Scotti being sick, but I planned on spending the next few days worshipping every inch of her beautiful body, starting with tonight.

Twenty Seven

Scotti

Mason wasn't kidding. We christened the hell out of every part of his house… OUR house. I never knew sex and love and relationships could be this incredible. When we first got home we barely got inside the door before Mason was picking me up and walking me into the kitchen. I was confused at first about what he was doing until he set me down on top of the table and slowly started removing my shirt. Sex on top of the table… I was all in for that.

Once we were done there we moved on to the floor of the living room. Although we said we were going to christen all of the furniture, I was perfectly fine with the floor and technically the couch has already been christened once before. Since we were already completely naked there was no time wasted. Mason slammed inside of me and within seconds I was having another incredible orgasm. Of course all of them with Mason are.

Once we were done, we laid there and caught our breath for a minute. Mason then picked me up, I wrapped my legs around him and he moved us into the bedroom. As soon as we closed the door I was pushed up against it and he was pushing himself inside of me, fucking me harder than I have ever been fucked in my entire life.

We pretty much did this day after day for the next four days. When we weren't making love, which wasn't often, we were holding each other, talking about anything and everything and just enjoying our life as husband and wife. By the end of those days, I was feeling more exhausted yet happier than I ever have.

We crashed in bed together, holding each other like we always do, when I suddenly woke up in a panic. My heart was racing, I was having trouble breathing and I felt incredibly nauseous. I slowly got up, not wanting to wake up Mason, but as soon as I stood up I immediately fell to the floor, knocking some stuff off the night stand causing a loud crashing sound.

"Scotti?" I heard Mason say in a sleepy voice, but I couldn't answer. I heard some shifting then heard Mason yell. "Scotti!" Mason was by my side, wiping my hair off my sweat soaked face and asking me over and over if I could hear him. I could, but I was having a hard time figuring out how to respond.

"Please, I need someone here immediately. My wife has collapsed and she has cancer." I looked over and could see Mason on the phone. The look on his face was a fear I have never seen before and all I wanted to do was hold him and tell him everything was going to be okay. Before I knew it, he was back by my side, kissing my face and telling me I was going to be fine… but I wasn't. I have read about the process of dying. This was just the beginning and I knew it was not going to get any better.

I slowly opened my eyes and looked around at the unfamiliar room I was in. It took a few minutes for me to remember that I was in the hospital. Before the ambulance even made it to our house I had completely passed out. I vaguely remember waking up once in the ambulance, but otherwise everything is pretty much a blur.

"Baby?" I heard Mason quietly say. I looked over to my left and he was looking at me with red and swollen eyes.

"I'm so sorry, Mason." I said, barely getting it out with how dry my throat was.

"Shhh, don't say you're sorry. You have nothing to be sorry for." He kissed my forehead then put a cup with a straw to my mouth, "Here, take a drink. It's just water."

I lifted my head enough to take a small sip than slowly laid it back down. My head felt like it weighed a million pounds. "How are you feeling?" He asked me.

"Like I am dying," I said jokingly, but judging by the look on Mason's face, now was definitely not the time for that, "Sorry, Mason. I just feel really tired. What happened?"

"You collapsed and couldn't breathe. By the time we got to the hospital you were out cold. Apparently, you were severely dehydrated and your oxygen levels were low so the doctors hooked you up to an IV and started you on oxygen. You are definitely not as pale as you were when we first got here."

"That's good." I could hear the bit of optimism from Mason and I did appreciate it.

"You are going to be fine, Scotti." Mason said, almost in a whisper.

I looked at him and gave him a weak smile, "No, I'm not, honey. I have talked to Dr. Hammond and done a lot of reading and I know this is just the start of what's to come."

He quickly stood up, ran his hands through his hair then grabbed my hand, "Please, don't say that! This is just a minor setback."

By this time the tears were falling down my face. I wanted to be optimistic like he was, I really did, but I also didn't want to fool myself. I knew what was coming. "Mason, please don't. You knew this was coming."

"Yes, but it wasn't supposed to happen this soon!" He yelled, startling me, "I'm sorry, I'm not yelling at you. I am just yelling at the situation."

I kissed his hand, "I know. I'm not saying I am dying tomorrow. I am just saying this is part of the process. This is how it happens. I am still going to have some good days, at least I hope so, but I am also going to have really bad days."

His tears were rolling down his face and as I tried to wipe them away they were flowing out even harder. He leaned in and kissed my forehead and cheeks over and over, crying the entire time. "Mason, are you sure you want to put yourself through this?" Fuck, that was the wrong thing to say.

He stopped kissing me and gave me a look that told me I should have really kept my mouth shut again. "Are you fucking kidding me, Scotti?" He got up then walked over to another chair that had his jacket lying across it.

I slowly sat up, "Where are you going?"

"I am just going to get some air." He said with a hint of anger. He put his jacket on then walked over to the side of my bed. "You have got to stop questioning this, stop questioning me. I love you Scotti. Until death do us part, remember?"

I nodded my head, now angry with myself, "I don't know why I said that again, it was stupid. I am so sorry."

He leaned down and kissed, "I'm not upset with you, I promise, I am just going to take a little walk. I will be back in just a few minutes."

I nodded, knowing that he needed to get out of this room for a few minutes and I didn't blame him a bit. I wish I could get up and take a walk too.

I watched him walk out and as soon as the door closed behind him, the tears began. I really do have to stop questioning him. He has proven time and time again that he loves me and wants to be with me no matter what. All I want to do is protect him from this pain but I just need to let go of that, because nothing I do could help that a bit. I laid my head down, closed my eyes and thought of nothing but the last few days I had with my husband. I fell in love so fast and so hard and even though he is going to be going through incredible pain when I am gone, I am so thankful that I no longer have to go through this alone.

Twenty Eight

Mason

Even though it was the middle of the night, there was quite a bit of activity in the hospital. I walked down the hallway and out the front door and saw a large tree in the grassy knoll and decided to sit there. It was cold outside but I needed to be somewhere where nobody would bother me. My wife was dying and I was sitting outside, freezing my ass off in the middle of the night, under a fucking tree.

I didn't want to be away from Scotti for very long so I cleared my head a bit then headed back upstairs to her room. When I walked in, her head was turned away from me and as I got closer to her I realized that she was asleep. I pulled up a chair next to her bed, put her hand in mine and did nothing but stare at her beautiful face. I feel like I have known her all my life and even though we just met, I can hardly remember my life without her in it. I keep hoping that some miracle is going to happen and this magic medicine is going to appear and cure her, but I know that is just wishful thinking. Cancer is a fucking bitch and even though Scotti is one of the most thoughtful and beautiful woman to ever be in existence, this fucking cancer is not going to spare her life. Since I have met her, I have been looking up cancer related stories on the internet and the suffering that people go through because of this horrendous disease is hard to fathom. I haven't lived under a rock, I know about cancer and know it kills thousands and thousands of people every single year but until Scotti, I never really KNEW about cancer. As much as I wish it wasn't true, I know Scotti is not going to survive this much longer. My only prayer now is that when she does die, she dies peacefully.

I lean into her and gently kiss her forehead, being careful not to wake her up. I quietly walk over to the other side of the room and grab a blanket, and then go back to my chair next to her bed. It is not an ideal sleeping arrangement, but I am going to touch her and kiss her and be as close to her as I possibly can for as long as this piece of shit disease allows me to. I put the blanket over me, hold her hand again then lay my head next to her. Before I close my eyes, I say a silent prayer to God that he will give us a little more time before he takes her. I know it won't be much, but I still need more. A tear falls down my face and I stare at Scotti until my eyes can no longer stay open, then before I know it I am falling fast asleep.

"Honey? Are you awake?" I hear the sweet voice of my wife but I am in complete darkness. I feel a light tugging on my hair, "honey?"

I lay there for a minute, not really sure if what I am hearing is a dream then quickly realize I fell asleep next to Scotti in the hospital and I am quickly jumping up, knocking over my chair and startling her. "Fucking hell Mason, what is wrong with you?" She yells.

I am trying to adjust my eyes to the light while willing my heart rate to slow down to a normal pace, "Sorry baby, you scared me. Are you okay?" My voice sounds hoarse and tired.

"I'm fine. A lot better than you it seems." She said with a smirk.

"I'm sorry, I guess I forgot for a minute where I was." I picked my chair up then sat back down and took her hand in mine and kissed it, "how are you feeling today?"

She kisses my hands back, "Good. I am ready to go home. Dr. Hammond said I would be able to leave this afternoon."

What the hell? "You saw the doctor this morning?"

She nodded her head, "Yeah. He was in here about a half hour ago. You were snoring away and I didn't want to wake you up."

"Scotti, always wake me up for something like that, please." I pleaded to her.

"Of course, sorry. I just wanted you to get your sleep. It was a rough night for you." She said with slight sadness in her voice.

"I don't mean to sound upset, I just don't want to miss anything." Especially anything the doctor has to say. She nodded her head in understanding. "So, what did he say?"

"Just that I need to take it easy and make sure I am getting a lot of sleep and he gave me a prescription for some pain medicine."

"Wait, are you in pain?" I know she felt a little tired and weak but she never said anything about pain.

She shook her head, "Not really, yet. He said that further along I will probably be experiencing a little pain and he just wanted me to have them for when that time comes."

The sadness in her voice is crushing me. She wants to be strong but as these things start happening and the process gets further along, I know it's going to be harder and harder for her to remain positive. I move myself on to her bed and pull her up against me, "We will handle this together, as things come along."

I feel her nodding her head then sniffle so I break away from her so I can look into her eyes. They are red and wet but she is working hard at not letting those tears fall. I lean into her and kiss her mouth and she kisses me back. "I love you, Mason," She tells me quietly.

"I love you too, baby," I tell her. I pull her back into my chest and hold her, loving the feeling of her head over my heart and her tiny arms wrapped around me. I am ready to get her home, into our own bed and just hold her some more. I kiss her again then jump up to grab her clothes so she can get dressed. I am looking around this small room, thankful that we are leaving but knowing that no matter how much I don't want it to be, we will be returning in the not so distant future, and suddenly I am back to feeling sad again.

Twenty Nine

Scotti

I love the outdoors and since I met Mason, I have fallen in love with his backyard. There really wasn't a lot to it but it is a good size and private and relaxing. I have decided that I am going to make some sort of garden of flowers back here, give the yard a little feminine touch. Mason ran to the garden supply store to get me some flowers and soil while I am using a small shovel to turn the dirt in a small area.

I have been home from the hospital for a week now and Mason has been treating me like I am a porcelain doll. It feels so good to be loved but I was feeling a little claustrophobic and needed a little space. When I came outside to take a breather, that is when I started looking around and came up with the idea to make this garden. It not only gets me out of the house but it gives me something to do as opposed to sitting inside the house and wondering what day I will die.

I continue digging when a sudden sharp pain hits me in the stomach so bad, I can't do anything but drop my shovel and double over in pain. I have never felt anything like this before and I am praying that it does not get any worse. I breathe through the pain, begging God to make it stop, and finally, after what seemed like an hour, the sharpness of the pain subsides.

I fall to my knees and bury my face in my hands, allowing myself this moment of weakness because after that pain I deserve it and also because my husband isn't home to witness it. I try to share all of this with Mason but I can see how much this is taking a toll on him and I don't want him any more upset than he already is.

I hear a car door close in the distance and I know it is Mason getting home. I quickly wipe my face, find the shovel I dropped and start my digging again. I can still feel some tenderness but the worst of it is over, for now anyways. I hear the sliding glass door open so I look up and see my sexy as hell husband filling up the doorway with his hot body and his incredible smile, "Hi honey, how was flower shopping?" I ask him.

He chuckles then shakes his head while walking towards me, "Let's just say that next time you want flowers for a garden, you are going with me to pick them out," he stops right in front of me and looks down in to my eyes, "I don't know the first thing about flowers so I hope I got what you want."

He is so fucking adorable, "I am sure they will be perfect. Thank you, Mason." He started to kneel down next to me and I looked away from him then started digging. I felt his hand on my chin, pulling my face over to look at him and when our eyes met, I smiled.

"What's wrong?" He asked me, while still holding his hand on my chin.

"Nothing's wrong honey. I have just been digging and it's getting a little warm. I am going to take a break in just a minute." I tried to turn my head back but he was holding me where I couldn't.

"Scotti, I am going to ask you again. What. Is. Wrong?" He never takes his eyes off me.

I took a deep breath then let it out, "It was nothing major. I just had a bit of pain in my stomach briefly. It was the first time I felt that but it's gone now."

"A bit of pain?" He asked, acting like he didn't believe me, instantly pissing me off.

"Yes, Mason, a bit of pain. Just drop it!" I push his hand off my chin then turn to continue my digging and Mason stands up and slowly walks in to the house without saying a word. FUCK! All he is doing is trying to help me and I instantly act like a bitch to him just because he asked me a question, a question that I gave a false answer to.

I jump up and run into the house. As soon as I get into the door I see Mason standing at the counter in the kitchen with his back turned towards me. "It was more than just a bit of pain." I tell him. He hasn't turned to look at me yet but I can tell by his body language that he heard me. "It was a horrible pain. A pain like I have never felt before and it took everything I had inside of me to not scream. I can't tell you how long it lasted, I just don't know. I do know it felt like it was never going to end." He still has not turned to look at me but he dropped his head, not liking what he was hearing. I slowly walk up behind him but don't touch him. "I was playing it off as nothing because I know how much you worry and I am sorry. I should have told you immediately and I especially should not have snapped at you just for being concerned." I put my arms around his waist and pressed my cheek up against his back, "I love you, Mason. Please don't hate me."

Mason turned around and before I could even look at him he was pulling me tightly into his chest, "Scotti, don't ever think for one second I could ever hate you. That will never happen. I love you so much. I know I can't make this go away but I am here for you through everything. I just don't want you to hide it from me."

"I know, I just don't want to be such a burden. I also don't want you upset."

"You are and never will be a burden, baby. I hate that you have to go through this and it hurts me when you are hurting but I want to know and I want to help you in any way I can, even if it's just holding you until it passes." He is continuing to hold me tight but with each word he speaks, that hold is getting a little tighter, but he is being careful to not squeeze too tight. I could live forever in his arms.

He loosens up his grip, enough for me to lift my head and look up at him. My sight is a little blurry from the tears but I can still see his red and watery eyes. I lift myself towards him and kiss him on the lips. He immediately starts kissing me back and before I know it, he is lifting me up so I can wrap my legs around his waist. "Please make love to me, Mason."

He freezes. We have not had sex since I went into the hospital, even though the doctor said we could if I felt good enough to. He is still holding me so I put my hands on each side of his face, "Honey, it's okay. I feel good right now."

He leans in so his forehead is touching mine, "I am scared to hurt you." He says, so quietly that even this close I almost couldn't hear him.

"You won't hurt me, Mason. You could never hurt me." I tell him.

He stands there, thinking about it for a minute then slowly walks us into the bedroom, never putting me down and never taking his eyes off of me. Once we get to the bed he slowly sits me down, then gets down on his knees in front of me and grabs my hands, "If at any moment, you are feeling anything but complete pleasure, tell me and I will stop immediately."

I nod my head, "Okay."

"Promise me Scotti. I don't want you to ever have a memory of us making love with anything but happiness."

I nod my head again.

"Promise me." He says again.

"I promise." I smile at him and I finally get a smile out of him. He slowly starts removing my top and as soon as he gets it off, he is kissing my stomach, my chest, breasts and neck. There is no better feeling than making love to my husband but the feelings I have inside when he is just kissing me is out of this world. I am so in love with this man and for the next couple of hours, he slowly but beautifully shows me just how in love he is with me too.

Thirty

Mason

"Son of a bitch!" I should have known that being away from my company for this long was going to end up biting me in the ass.

"Mason, what's going on?" She asks me, after I throw my cell phone down on the kitchen counter.

"Just shit happening at work."

"So, go take care of it." She says like it's no big deal.

I shake my head, "I don't want to leave you."

"Honey, I hate to break it to you but I lived a lot of years without you so I think I can handle a few hours."

I know she's right. It's not a matter of her not being able to take care of herself but more me not wanting to lose precious time with her, "I know you can baby, I just… the guys can handle it."

She walks up to me so we are standing toe to toe. If I wasn't so much taller than her, her nose would be touching mine, but instead she has to look up at me, "Mason, go take care of your work stuff, then get home and we can spend the afternoon doing something. I am going crazy and need to get out of this house."

"You can go with me." I tell her, hoping she will agree but knowing better.

"No thank you. I will take the time to take a shower and get dressed. I will be ready to head out as soon as you are done and back home."

I think about it for a minute, knowing if I don't go fix this paperwork it will consume my every thought until it is fixed, "Okay fine, I will go take care of it as quickly as possible then get right home. Then we will go do whatever you would like to do."

She smiled widely, lifts herself up to kiss me then heads to the sink to clean up our breakfast dishes. I run to the bedroom to get dressed, not wanting to waste any time, so I can get back to my wife and hopefully salvage most of the day.

This is definitely not going as planned. I have now been here for over two hours trying to fix this shit storm that my guys created during my absence and I am getting more pissed off by the minute. At this rate, I will never get out of here, which means that is one less day that I have with my wife, and that thought is making me angrier. I am staring at these invoices, trying to make heads or tails of this shit when I hear my office door open. "The best thing you can do at this point is turn the fuck around and get the fuck out!" I yell, not even looking up from my work.

"You kiss your wife with that mouth?"

I shoot my head up and see my beautiful girl standing inside my office with a huge smile on her face. I jump up and run over to her. "Scotti, what are you doing here?" I ask, while hugging her like I haven't seen her in days.

"I figured you were super busy and I was bored at home so I thought I would come down here and see if there is anything I could help you with.

Also, I have never seen your office before." She was looking around at the bare walls, probably decorating it in her head as she was speaking.

"Baby, I love that you came down here and I love that you want to help and all but… how did you get here?"

"I called a cab," She said shrugging her shoulders, while still walking around surveying my office.

"You called a cab? Scotti, are you insane? You should have called me and I would have come and picked you up." I have been in cabs many times but for some reason I was not thrilled about my wife riding in one without me there.

She stopped walking then turned to look at me, or should I say glare at me. "Mason, I have been in plenty of cabs over the years so stop being so damn overprotective, and besides, you left this behind."

She lifts her hand that is holding my cell phone. I ran out of the house so fast that I forgot to grab it off the counter. As much as I want to yell and forbid her to ever get into another cab, I really don't have a valid argument since she had no way of getting a hold of me anyway. "You're right, I'm wrong, I am being very overprotective but only because I love you," I put my arms around her and kiss the top of her head, "but will you please not ride in any more cabs alone?"

She giggled then looked up at me, "That was tough for you, wasn't it?"

"You have no idea." I told her, never feeling good about admitting that I am wrong.

She thinks about it for a second. "Okay Mason, I won't ride in a cab alone ever again, I promise."

"Thank you, my love." I kiss her again and she steps away from me.

"So, is there anything I can help you with?" She asks me.

I nod at her, tired of driving myself crazy with this one invoice, "No, to be honest, I am so sick of looking at this shit. Let me get stuff put away and we will get out of here." I turned and walked to my desk, "so, what do you want to do today?" I ask her, just as I sit down in my chair.

"Well, there is something I have really wanted to do since I met you." She started walking towards me very slowly with a very seductive look on her face and I admit I was intrigued.

I lifted one eyebrow, "Oh, really? And would that be, Mrs. Shaw?"

She turns my chair so I am facing her then sits on my lap, straddling me. I don't know what her plan is but I hope like hell she isn't just teasing me because I am already hard as a rock. She scoots closer to me, and I can tell by the look on her face, that she knows exactly what she is doing to me. She smiles sweetly then gently places her hand on my jeans right on top of my incredibly hard cock. "Scotti…" I said, not able to say anything more.

"Mason," she whispered then kissed me gently.

"Tell me what you want, Scotti." I said, barely able to speak.

She took her hand off my pants then smiled, "Lift me on to your desk and fuck me hard, so whenever you are sitting here working, I am all you can think about."

My mouth dropped open. My woman has a kinky side and fuck if that doesn't turn me the hell on!

Thirty One

Scotti

I blame the fact that I am dying for becoming so bold with Mason but in all honesty, if I would have met him and had not been dying, I probably would still be this way. I can't help it. He definitely brings out the nymphomaniac in me. I have never felt so turned on by a man in my life and Mason can bring that out of me with just a look.

The look of shock on his face is hilarious and I am trying to keep my expression as serious as possible when what I really want to do is burst out laughing. Now, if I did that, I have a feeling I would be seriously bruising my husband's ego, making him think I am joking and not really wanting this from him.

He slowly starts to get out of his chair, putting his hands on my ass to hold me. As soon as he is almost completely standing I wrap my legs around his waist. I am waiting for him to set me down on his desk but instead he stands there, staring into my eyes and not saying a word.

"Mason, what's wrong?"

"Every time we get to this point I am afraid of doing something to hurt you."

"What? Mason, what are you talking about?"

"I know the doctor says these issues you are having lately are part of the process but what if I end up doing some serious damage or what if I am hurting you and you don't tell me because you are afraid of hurting my feelings." He never looks away from me the entire time and I can see the love he has for me, right inside his beautiful brown eyes.

"You won't hurt me Mason. The doctor said that making love is okay."

He gives me a slight smirk, "I am sure it is, but you, my little minx, are asking me to fuck you silly, in my office, on my desk."

I smile back at him, happy that he is able to joke around, "You're right, I am asking that. And I expect you to deliver, otherwise I may need to go out and find myself a different husband."

He laughed hard while still continuing to hold me, "Oh baby, you will never be able to find another person on the face of this Earth that will love you as much as I do. That is a fact."

I knew he was right. Mason loved me like nobody has nor ever will. I pulled his face to me and slammed my lips on to his. His words ignited a fire that was already burning hot. Instead of pulling back, he set me down on his desk and wrapped his hands in my hair and kissed me with such intensity that I knew my lips would be bruised, a bruising that I more than welcome.

I reached down and started unbuckling his belt as he was yanking at my shirt, ripping it open instead of unbuttoning it. It seemed like it took hours to get our clothes off each other when really it was just a minute. Mason stopped kissing me and took a step back. He was completely naked and so was I and all I could do was stare at his incredible body. We were both breathing heavily and just when I was going to ask him if something was wrong I looked deeper into his eyes and saw it. He was studying me. He was taking a mental picture of every single part of me from my couple of freckles I have on my leg up to my small scar above my eye. I could see the passion in his eyes as he looked over my body but I knew that wasn't the only thing and instead of being self-conscious and insecure, I didn't move a muscle. I let him have this time. I let him memorize everything. This is something Mason needed and I was not about to take this away from him.

He spent several minutes looking me over. I was almost afraid to breathe and my limbs were starting to cramp up from being so still. "God, Scotti, you are so beautiful," Mason said in a whisper.

I smiled at him but didn't say anything in return. He finally took the couple of steps back over to me, put his hands on each side of my face again and pulled my lips to his. He didn't kiss me right away, instead just held his lips on mine for a few seconds, then gently and slowly began kissing me. I felt him pull me closer to him, wrapping my legs around his waist and next thing I knew, he was slowly pushing himself inside of me. This is my favorite part of having sex with Mason. Don't get me wrong, I love all of it, but that initial moment, when he first enters my body, is the best feeling I have ever had.

I stopped kissing him and dropped my head back. Mason was going so slow, making this feel like heaven. I lifted my head and as soon as my eyes met his, he started moving. Holy hell this felt amazing! I grabbed on to his shoulders and tightened my legs around his waist and he had his hands holding my hips tight.

He started moving even faster and I couldn't be quiet any longer. I was moaning so loud that I knew if any of his guys were outside the door there is no doubt they were hearing me.

My hands were getting sweaty and slipping so I wrapped my arms around his neck and started moving with him. With each thrust my moans were getting louder and soon Mason's volume was matching mine. I didn't even feel a build-up of my orgasm. One minute I was panting and moaning and the next I was screaming in pleasure. I was still screaming when Mason started yelling out his orgasm, making me yell even louder. I loved the sounds he made when he was coming.

He continued moving inside of me but gradually slowed down until we were both at a complete stop. My ass was killing me from this weird position I had on the desk and my legs were cramping but I couldn't move. It was almost like we were both paralyzed, but in a good way. There had to be gallons of sweat between us so whatever paperwork Mason was working on before I got here, was going to be stuck to my ass as soon as I got up.

I started laughing at the image of that, making Mason lift his head and give me a strange look, "Definitely not the reaction I was expecting."

I laughed even harder, trying to catch my breath and even though I couldn't get out exactly what I was laughing at, Mason started laughing too. I buried my face in his neck, continuing to laugh until the giggles had finally passed. "I swear I wasn't laughing at you, Mason. I just had a mental image of… oh never mind, it was stupid."

He didn't question me on it. He just stared at me with a huge grin on his face looking every bit satisfied after our office rendezvous. "Baby, please tell me that met your expectations."

I shook my head, "No, that exceeded my expectations," he smiled again, even wider than before, "I think we get better every time."

He nodded, "That is for damn sure."

I chuckled as Mason slowly started lifting me from the desk and sure enough there was a paper stuck to my ass. Mason quickly grabbed it and threw it on the ground. He was still inside of me and even though he wasn't as hard as before, I could still feel him and now I was ready for round two. "Mason, can you take us over to your office chair?"

He looked confused but immediately sat down on the chair, still holding me so I was now straddling him. I think he thought I was hurting so as soon as he sat, he was moving my hair out of my face and looking me over. I slowly started moving in his lap and within just a couple of seconds he realized what I was doing. He moved his hands down to my ass and pulled me even closer, "Fuck baby."

I continued moving until I felt myself running out of steam and as if Mason could sense that, he started helping me along, moving his hips up and down. Neither of our orgasms took nearly as long this time as they did last time and before I knew it, we were both yelling our pleasure together.

I immediately collapsed to Mason's chest, burying my face in his neck, enjoying his soap and sweat smell. This man has made me the happiest woman alive and I know, if I am to die tomorrow, I will die the happiest I have ever been in my life.

Thirty Two

Mason

This morning, for the first time ever, I woke up having a panic attack. My heart was racing, I could barely breathe and for a moment I thought maybe I was having a heart attack. As soon as I looked over and could see my beautiful sleeping wife next to me, I started settling down, realizing that this was anxiety and nothing else. I don't remember if I was dreaming but I figure if I was, it was nothing good.

Each day that comes and goes, I know is another day closer to the end of Scotti's life and the thought is frightening. I have been alone for so long that one would think it would be easy to be alone again after only having her for a short time, but I don't know how I can possibly be on this Earth without her by my side. I am not proud of it, but I actually started thinking about ways I could take my own life, just so I don't have to be without her. I made the mistake of talking to Scotti about those feelings and she freaked out, begging me to continue living and to move on from her. I really hate when she says things like that. There will never be anyone else in my life, ever!

"Honey?" Scotti says in a sleepy voice, startling me. I look over at her and she can barely open her eyes, her hair is all over the place and she has never looked more beautiful. I lean into her and kiss her on the forehead.

"Sorry for waking you. Go back to sleep, baby."

"Okay," she said and within seconds she was sound asleep.

I quietly got out of bed, threw on some sweat pants and tiptoed out of the bedroom. When I got downstairs the sun was just barely starting to rise so the house was still pretty dark but instead of turning on any lights I walked over to the couch, sat down and stared at the empty wall in front of me. Losing Scotti consumes all my thoughts every single day. We have good times, smile, laugh, joke around, make love but with each of those things, I think about what it will be like to not have that anymore. Every smile she makes I try to memorize so I never forget how her eyes light up and her nose crinkles when she does it. Every time we make love I touch every single inch of her body to make sure I never forget how smooth her skin feels or how amazing she smells from head to toe. Every fucking thought is about that. I don't want it to be and when I tell myself I need to just live each day and deal with the rest later, I do that for about four seconds before I am right back to thinking about her death.

"Mason? Are you out here?" I hear Scotti say. Even though the sun has risen more, the house is still not lit up well.

I stand up from the couch and turn to see her standing there with a blanket wrapped around her body, "I'm by the couch baby." I walk over to her and when she sees me she gives me a look like she knows exactly what I have been thinking about. As soon as I reach her she opens her blanket, giving me a look at her gorgeous body, then wraps her arms around my waist and lays her head on my chest.

"I want to tell you to stop worrying and not think about it, but I know it won't do any good, because I am always thinking about it too." I can hear the sadness in her voice and it is breaking me down. She looks up at me, with tears running down her cheeks, "I can feel that I am getting weaker, that it is starting to take its toll. When we first got together I would go to bed every night, just praying for the next day but now, I just pray for the pain to be tolerable, because each morning that I open my eyes, I am feeling a little more off. Not terrible, just…off."

I have been noticing that she is getting slower in her movements, even when we were having sex at my office, she ran out of energy a lot faster than usual, but I didn't want to say anything, worrying that she would get upset. "Please tell me when you are feeling those things so I can help you. That is what I am here for. I love you and I want to take away as much burden as I possibly can."

"I know. I am trying. I feel like I am getting better at letting you know my feelings. It's just hard to be dependent on someone after so many years of not having anyone."

"I can understand that. I think that is something that is hard for both of us to do. I guess we are learning to depend on each other, together." I couldn't fault her for feeling that way. It was not easy for me either.

She nodded her head then steps away from me and walks over to the window. The sun is up now. Light is pouring in the windows and hitting my wife so perfectly that she literally looks like an angel standing here. She takes a deep breath then lets it out, still with her back to me. "What's wrong, baby?" I ask her.

She shakes her head but still doesn't turn around to look at me. I walk up behind her, gently put my arms around her body and lean down so my lips are right at her ear, "Remember? Tell me what you are feeling." I whisper to her.

She drops her head and begins sobbing then quickly turns around and wraps her arms around me, "I don't want to die, Mason! I want to live! I want to live and grow old with you! What if there is no heaven or memories of us? What if it hurts at the end? What if it's not peaceful like the doctors say it will be? This isn't fair!"

I don't know what to say. I want that more than anything too and if there was something I could do to change it, I would do it in a fucking heartbeat. I wrap my arms so tight around her little body that I fear I may break her, but I can't let her go. I know she said she wouldn't get upset anymore but with the changes in her body, how could she not? She needs to get this out instead of holding it in. She needs to cry and scream and if she really wants, she can break some more glasses. I can't help but think about what she just said.

Tears are falling down my face and I am silently asking myself those same questions. What if it does hurt at the end? How in the hell can I possibly fix that? I know that I will always have those memories of her but what if she is right. What if there is no heaven? I can't let myself go there. There has to be an amazing place that we all go to after we die, there just has to be. This beautiful and amazing woman is going to be ripped from my arms so I refuse to believe that she is going anywhere but to a beautiful and better place, a place where she will be at peace and cancer free and happy. A place that she shines as bright as the sun, because after all the shit she has endured in her life, she fucking deserves that.

Thirty Three

Scotti

I needed that breakdown. I had been trying to hold it in since the pan incident because I promised to stay positive, but I just couldn't stay positive anymore. I didn't want to show Mason how I was feeling because I knew it would upset him but I had to and I knew Mason would be right here to hold me and get me through it. I could feel his tears hitting my head and I could hear the sadness in his voice but I knew he needed to let it out just like I did, so I didn't say anything.

Once we were both done crying, he carried me to bed, wrapped his arms around me and we both fell asleep for a few hours, until the sound of my stomach growling woke us both up. While I was getting dressed, Mason ran to the kitchen to fix us some breakfast.

"It smells amazing in here." I told him, walking into the kitchen.

"I made some Belgian waffles and extra crispy bacon, just the way you like it," He said smiling as he removed a waffle from the waffle iron.

"Perfect. Bacon always makes everything better." He laughed as he walked towards me with a plate of food. I sat down at the kitchen table as he set the plate right in front of me. The syrup and two glasses of milk were already on the table so I loaded up my waffle with way too much syrup and dug in.

Mason sat down next to me with his plate, poured about two drops of syrup on his waffle then started to eat.

"What the hell is the point of that?" I asked him, pointing at his plate with my fork.

"The point of what?" He asked me with a mouth full of food.

"Putting hardly any syrup on your waffle, you might as well just leave it dry."

"I put just enough on there to give it a little syrupy flavor, that's all I need," he takes a drink of his milk then continues, "and what about you? You put so much syrup on yours that it has turned into mush. That's disgusting," he says, laughing.

"I happen to like it really wet."

"Oh, I like it really wet too, baby," he says while raising both eyebrows up and down.

I turn to look at him and start laughing. How does a conversation about syrup turn sexual? I shake my head then go back to eating as Mason just chuckles. We both continue eating in silence, both starving not only from working up an appetite with all our lovemaking yesterday but going back to sleep and getting up late. I finish my last bite, put my fork down and Mason is immediately taking both of our plates in to the kitchen. "So, since we didn't go out yesterday, is there something you would like to do today?" Mason asks.

I smile at him and nod, "Actually, yes, there is something I have wanted to do for quite a long time."

"Whatever you want to do," He says while washing the dishes.

I clap my hands and jump up, "Okay. Great! I will go get ready!" I start running up the stairs to the bedroom to put my shoes on. I have wanted to do this for so long, hopefully Mason will be on board with it.

"Are you out of your fucking mind, Scotti? No way!" We are sitting in the parking lot outside of the amusement park that I have wanted to go to my entire life but never got the chance. I asked Charlie once if we could go and he smacked me for daring to spend his money on something so juvenile.

"Why? It's just an amusement park. How bad can it be, Mason?" I didn't understand why he was getting so upset over a stupid amusement park.

"There are a million things we could be doing right now and watching you whirl around on a death defying contraption is not exactly at the top of the list."

"You mean us." I told him.

"Excuse me?"

"I said US, you and me will be whirling around together and not just on one... I want to ride all of them! I have always wanted to go to an amusement park! Now I get to share this experience with the love of my life," I smiled as sweet as I could but it didn't seem to be working.

He quickly started shaking his head, "There is no fucking way you are getting me on any of those rides. And there is certainly no way that I am allowing you to ride them either. There is no way that can be good for you!"

Yeah, like I am going to listen to that shit. I didn't realize my husband would be so afraid of a roller coaster but putting that aside, telling me that he will not allow me to ride is something that can possibly get him smacked. "Mason, I will listen to you on most things but you will not talk to me like I am your child and you certainly will not tell me what I can and cannot do!" He was looking at me like he was trying to figure out something to say but instead kept his mouth shut… which was exactly what I should have done too. "Besides, who cares if they are death defying. I am dying anyways! What is the worst that can happen?" SHIT! SHIT! SHIT! That was a stupid thing to say.

He jumped out of his truck and slammed the door so hard that the entire thing shook. I jumped out to chase after him, "Mason, wait!" I yelled to him, but he was not slowing down. I kept yelling his name and realized I was making quite a scene, but I really didn't give a shit at this point. Right now, all I wanted was to get my husband to forgive me. "Please, honey, I'm sorry. Stop running away from me!" He stopped and instead of continuing to walk to him, I stopped too. He turned around and the look on his face wasn't one of a man that was pissed off, I had hurt him, and now my heart hurt too.

Neither one of us moved for a minute which was getting us nowhere. Since this was my fault, I slowly started walking towards him. Mason didn't move nor did he take his eyes off of mine. I got to him and grabbed his hand and kissed it, "I say those things because I am scared and making jokes is how I cope. It is wrong of me and I'm sorry. I should not have said that."

"No, you shouldn't have. Especially after the morning we had."

"I know." I said, ashamed of myself for making those kind of jokes.

I was still holding his hand so he was able to pull me to him and we both wrapped our arms around each other. I love the feeling of being in Mason's arms, even if it is in the middle of a sidewalk. "You don't really want to get on those rides do you?" He said into my neck.

I chuckled, "Yes, I really do."

He sighed then kissed my neck and pulled away from me. "Okay. Fine. I guess there is no better time than the present. I am not happy about it but if it's something you want, you know I can't possibly say 'no' to you, but don't think for a minute I will be getting on one of those things with you."

He smiled then grabbed my hand and walked back towards the entrance of the park. I never would have thought my big tough husband was so afraid of roller coasters but I knew this was something I had to do. After I ride my first one I may hate it then stop but I want to at least experience it once. Now I just need to convince Mason to experience it with me.

Thirty Four

Mason

I thought my heart was going to jump out of my skin. Once we got inside and Scotti saw how big those rides really were, I saw the blood drain right from her face. For a brief moment, I thought that meant that she would change her mind. NO. SUCH. LUCK. She got a huge smile on her face then started running towards the biggest roller coaster that was at that park. I chased after her, not with excitement, more with panic at her over exerting herself. Once we got to the line for the ride I opted to sit on the bench. Scotti was trying everything to get me to go on with her but I refused.

This was never anything that interested me nor will it ever. After a few begging words, and even a few times of being called a pussy, Scotti finally gave up and got in line by herself. Once she got to the front of the line she turned to make sure I was still watching and held two thumbs up with a huge smile on her face. My heart started racing as I saw her small body, sitting in a huge metal box, speeding around a track while the sounds of screams and laughter were coming from her. As much as I hated her doing this, I couldn't help but smile at her happiness.

Once the car stopped, I walked over to the exit area and within just a few seconds Scotti came barreling down the ramp. She saw me and smiled then ran over and threw herself into my arms, "That was awesome! I am definitely riding that one again before we leave!" Her enthusiasm was contagious and I couldn't help but start smiling with her.

"I figured you must have liked it. I could hear your excitement down here." I kissed her then grabbed her hand to start walking towards another ride.

"Liked it? I loved it! Thank you, Mason." She squeezed my hand and smiled at me.

"Thank me for what?"

"Thank you for bringing me here. I know it doesn't seem like a huge deal but this is something I have always wanted to do."

"I know I freaked out a little in the truck but you know I will do anything to make you happy," I stopped walking then pulled her face to mine, "even if it means watching you flip upside down over and over again."

She pushed her face in to mine and started kissing me, probably a little more than she should have considering all the kids around us, but I didn't care. I was going to enjoy each and every one of these moments as long as I could. She pulled away and smiled widely at me, "Mason, I love that you will do anything for me so do you think you could do something else?"

"Baby, I told you I would do anything." And I meant it, or so I thought.

She jumped up and down and started clapping, "Excellent. Then you will ride the next one with me."

I shook my head, "Fuck no, I will do anything but that!" Didn't we already have this conversation?

"Okay, how about we just have our day together here. Eat some incredibly fattening food, play some games, I will ride some more rides by myself but before we leave I would like you to ride that first one with me, just one time. Please, please, please!" I cannot believe I am even considering this but making Scotti happy was seriously my number one priority.

I took a deep breath and slowly let it out, "Fine," she practically started screaming, "to just the one ride, before we leave."

She threw her arms around me and squeezed me so tight you would have thought I just handed her a million dollar check or something, "Thank you, Mason."

I kissed the top of her head then we grabbed each other's hands and continued walking. I guess riding on that thing was a small price to pay to see this smile on my wife's face, and I was willing to make that sacrifice. I mean really, how bad could it be?

"Oh my God! Make it stop!" Well, I found out exactly how bad it could be since I am now currently puking my guts out in a garbage can in, thankfully, an almost empty parking lot. Every once in a while I think I hear Scotti giggling but when I look up her face shows nothing but concern so I am either imagining it or she is just that good at hiding it.

"Honey, is there anything I can do for you? Rub your back? Anything?" Scotti is standing near me, but not too close. The sound of me getting sick is making her gag so she is keeping her distance, while trying to be helpful and loving.

"No, I will be fine, just give me a minute."

"You said that over thirty minutes ago. We really need to get you home." She walks behind me and gently grabs my arm, "come on, I will drive."

I immediately stop and shake my head, "Hell no! The last time you drove we almost died!"

She puts her hand on her hip and raises her eyebrows, "Really, Mason, now you're just being a drama queen. Just get in the truck. I will take it slow and easy and get us home safe with no problem. I promise."

I knew we had no choice. There is no way I could drive like this. I don't remember the last time I ever got this sick but after eating all the shit we did today then going on that ride with Scotti was definitely the worst idea ever. Everything we ate, plus everything I have eaten for the past thirty years, has decided to come up.

I put my hand into hers and we slowly made our way to the truck. Scotti unlocked it, and then opened the passenger side door for me to climb in. As soon as I got inside the truck, I immediately reclined my seat back. Scotti got inside the truck and turned it on, "Honey, do you want me to stop anywhere on the way home and get you some crackers and 7-Up?"

"No. Please, let's just get home," I closed my eyes, hoping like hell that I could make it all the way home without having Scotti pull over. I felt the truck start moving and instead of panicking, which would be the right thing to do after the last time I let Scotti drive, the movement started relaxing me and before I knew it, I was falling into a deep sleep.

Thirty Five

Mason

Riding on a roller coaster was something that was never on my list of things to do but since Scotti asked me, I couldn't possibly say no. I hated every second of it. I was trying to keep a smile on my face knowing how much fun Scotti was having, but it was not an easy task. Where did I go wrong on all this? Well, I ate an obscene about of fried goodness before I went on that ride which was not the smartest thing I have ever done. The second the ride was over I was running to a trash can, burying my head in it and throwing up like I have never thrown up before. I was worried Scotti would run away and be disgusted. She did gag a couple of times but she still stood next to me and comforted me by rubbing my back, and occasionally laughing.

Once I was done we made our way to the parking lot, where luckily there were more trash cans for me to stick my head in. I had never been so sick in my entire life and it all happened because of one fucking roller coaster. Shit, I really am a pussy!

Even after everything that happened last night, I was feeling pretty well rested. I reached over to pull my wife against me, loving the feeling of her body, but she wasn't there and the sheets were cool. I shot up, worried that something was wrong and was instantly hit with the smell of bacon. Damn, that smells good. I went into the bathroom, did my business which included brushing my teeth about ten times and made my way downstairs.

As soon as I hit the kitchen I stopped dead in my tracks. My wife, my beautiful fucking amazing wife, was standing at the stove, flipping bacon in a pan, in nothing but my shirt and some fuzzy socks. I clear my throat, not wanting to scare her and cause her to burn herself, and she looks over her shoulder and smiles. I walk up behind her, wrap my arms around her and bury my face in her neck, "Good morning, baby."

"Good morning. How are you feeling?" She asked, while still fixing our food.

"Starving now that I have smelled breakfast," I kissed her on the cheek, "you should have woke me up, I would have made breakfast for us."

She pulled the last piece of bacon out of the pan, set it on a paper towel then turned towards me and wrapped her arms around my neck, "You needed your sleep. Besides, I like doing it. I feel like I am actually taking care of you for once."

She kissed my lips gently then slowly slipped her tongue in my mouth, turning me on. I picked her up, set her on the counter and started unbuttoning her shirt, "Mason, what the hell are you doing? One of these days I would like to actually finish cooking you breakfast and we actually eat it."

I got her shirt open, pulled one of her nipples in my mouth and gently started sucking on it. Scotti let out a moan then put her hands into my hair and squeezed. I stopped sucking and lifted my head, "We can stop. I would never want to deny you the chance to cook and eat breakfast."

She grabbed a hold of my hair again, "Don't you dare stop Mason Shaw! The fucking bacon can wait!"

I chuckled then finished removing her shirt. I took a step back and looked at my wife, sitting on the counter in our kitchen wearing nothing but socks, and I thought I was going to come just from the sight of her. "Wrap your legs around me." I told her. I walked over to the wall between the kitchen and living room, pushed my sweat pants down with one hand while holding Scotti with the other, gently shoved her up against the wall and pushed my cock inside of her. There was no need for any foreplay, she was soaked.

"Oh God, Mason." She moaned out.

I kissed her gently on the lips, "I love you so much, Scotti," I was moving in and out of slowly, "you have made me the happiest I have ever been in my entire life," a little faster, "and no matter how much or how little time we have with each other, I will never regret one minute of it. You are my soul mate."

I saw a tear rolling down the side of Scotti's face and I kissed it as it hit her cheek then kissed her forehead then her lips. She started moaning into my mouth and her legs were squeezing me tighter, so I moved faster. I was so close and I knew she was too. Our bodies were slick so she held on tighter. Just as I reached down to touch her clit, she came with a loud scream. Before she was even finished, my orgasm hit and just when I didn't think our sex life could get any better, I realized I was dead wrong. I don't think I have ever come so hard in my life. Of course I think that each time we have sex.

We were both coming down from our orgasmic high, breathing heavily and sweating like we were in a sauna. I still had her pinned up against the wall and our foreheads were together with our eyes closed. When I was finally able to lift them open, her beautiful eyes were staring into mine and she was smiling, "Wow, Mason, that was incredible."

"It is always incredible with you and me. That is how I know we are meant to be." I kissed her slowly, deeply and could feel myself getting hard again. I walked us over to the living room and laid on the couch with Scotti on top of me. I had not even pulled out of her from the first time yet and wasn't sure if she would even have the energy to do this again but as soon as she started rocking her hips, I knew she wanted it just as much as I did. We kissed, made love, kissed some more and did nothing but worship each others' bodies. We did eventually eat, but that breakfast that my wife made quickly became our late afternoon lunch.

Thirty Six

Scotti

My life was a fairy tale. Well, it was almost a fairy tale. I had the most amazing husband that a person could possibly dream of. We lived in a beautiful home. And we sat on the beach at least three to four evenings a week to watch the sunset. The fact that Mason didn't try to stop me from doing that made me love him so much. The fact that he sat right next to me, held my hand, stroked my hair and watched with me, made me love him that much more.

I woke up this morning, feeling like things were going so great that nothing could ever bring me down. That was until I actually got out of bed. I was so weak I could hardly walk. Just going from the bed to the bathroom caused me to sweat like I had just run a marathon.

Part of the process.

Everything like this that I experience is just part of the process and when the time comes, that I can no longer handle it anymore, I will be given a sedative that will make me fall asleep and keep me comfortable until my body finally gives out.

I could hear Mason moving around downstairs and as much as I was not ready to have this talk with him, I knew that things were only going to get worse so I really needed to. I took time, getting cleaned up, dressed and looking somewhat presentable even though I felt like complete shit.

As I slowly made my way downstairs, I saw Mason sitting at the table, drinking some coffee and I knew as soon as he saw me he would freak out so I walked slowly, careful not to make myself known, but as soon as I got to the barstools, my legs gave out and I went crashing down, taking one of the stools with me.

Mason immediately jumped up and ran over to me, "Oh God, baby. Are you okay?" He asked me in a panic.

I nodded my head but didn't want to speak fearing that I might start crying. Mason lifted me up and carried me over to the couch, sitting down while cradling me in his lap. "I'm calling the doctor."

"No, Mason, it's not necessary. I'll be fine. I just need a little time." Time wasn't going to help me. Time was only going to make me worse. I felt myself tearing up but I wanted to be strong, I wanted to be like people I read about that say that they came to terms with their illness and are just living their lives. I want to be like that so much… but I'm not. I am still just as angry today as I was the day I was told there was nothing that could be done to help me. Actually, I am angrier because now I have this beautiful man, holding me in his arms, that doesn't deserve this pain. I couldn't hold it anymore, the tears started flowing so I laid my head on Mason's chest and just let them flow.

"Baby, are you in pain? Please talk to me. You're scaring me." I could hear the fear in his voice and that was absolutely crushing me.

"No, not really much pain at all, just really weak. I'm sorry for scaring you, Mason. I should have stayed upstairs until this passed."

"Hell no. Don't ever lock yourself away when you aren't feeling good. Just next time call for me and I will come help you." I nodded my head in his chest. "Is this… um… is this part of the process?" His voice was cracking when he asked that and as much as I wanted to tell him it wasn't there was no reason to lie to him. He is with me until the end, and unfortunately the end was near.

"Yes," I said in a whisper, and I immediately felt his body jolt, surprised that I had actually told him or maybe upset that his fear was a reality. "But I don't hurt much so I don't want any drugs. I think today is just one of the days that I need to rest."

"Of course, baby. Whatever you need." Mason kissed my head and held me tighter.

"I'm sorry, honey. I know we had made plans to visit the new art museum in town." I really was disappointed. I had never been to an art museum and I was really looking forward to it.

"Scotti, don't be sorry. You can't help it if you aren't feeling good. We will just lie around, watch movies, nap and cuddle all day."

This man is so perfect. Why couldn't we have crossed paths years ago? "I love you, Mason. Thank you."

"I love you, baby, more and more every day." We stayed like that for quite a while. I loved lying on Mason's chest and listening to his heartbeat. It was very relaxing. However, I knew the longer that I stalled, the harder this would be. I slowly started to sit up and couldn't believe how difficult it was just to do that. "Scotti, what are you doing? You need to rest."

"I will rest in a while, I promise, but first, we need to talk about some things." I took a deep breath and blinked several, willing my eyes to stay dry for now.

"Of course. What would you like to talk about?"

"Well, I think it's time we had the talk." I started choking up so I cleared my throat and continued, "it's time we had the talk about what to do when I die."

Thirty Seven

Mason

I knew this was coming. I didn't quite know it was coming today but I knew eventually we would have to discuss this. I swallowed, not understanding why she is choosing this moment to have the talk. "I know, baby, I really do, but why now, why today?"

She looked down then when she looked back at me I could see that she was holding in the tears, "Because honey, I don't have much more time." She is talking so quietly that I almost didn't hear her, in fact I was hoping I heard her wrong.

"What do you mean? Has the doctor said something that I didn't know about? Why do you say that, Scotti?" I am panicking and spitting out question after question at her, but I couldn't figure out why she wanted to do this today.

She was still sitting on my lap but she slowly turned her body so she was facing me, then put her hands on either side of my face, "Mason, honey, with the exception of the hospital when you were sleeping, I have never talked to the doctor without you since we have been together. It's just, today, the way I am feeling right now, I can just tell. I feel it."

"Everyone has rough days sometimes. Everyone feels a little weak and drained sometimes. That doesn't mean anything." A tear fell down my face but I refused to brush it away. I won't hide anything from her, not even tears.

"Mason, for me, it does mean something. For me, it means my body is starting to shut down. It means that this whole process crap that the doctors keep talking to us about is starting to happen and because it is, we need to figure things out, before I get even worse." Her body language was strong, but her voice was cracking and I knew this was hurting her so much. I know how I feel knowing she won't be here forever but I can't even imagine what it would be like to know that a disease inside your body is eating at you and is killing you. She says she is not strong but from what I see, she is the strongest person I have ever known.

I took another deep breath and as much as I wanted to argue, I couldn't. "Okay, baby, let's talk."

She smiled weakly at me then swallowed and wasn't speaking right away. I think a big fucking dose of reality has just hit us both. She looked like she was zoning out but I was just giving her whatever time she needed to get the words out. "Well, I think the main thing is what to do with me once I'm gone. I… I don't want to be buried in the ground. I have been thinking about this quite a bit and I think I want to be cremated, and maybe my ashes scattered in the ocean, at our beach."

Ever since we got together and especially since we got married, Scotti has been calling the place where we met 'our' beach. It is the exact place where we go and sit and watch the sunset several times a week. As far as we are both concerned, that place is magical so for her to want her ashes scattered there doesn't surprise me at all. "Okay," was all I could say. Whatever she wants is what she is going to get. Either way, whether it is in the ground or cremated, it's still going to be my wife that is no longer living.

She nodded her head, accepting my short answer knowing how uncomfortable this conversation is for both of us. "I think the only other thing is where it's going to happen."

"Where what is going to happen?" I was confused by this.

"Where I'm going to die, Mason."

"I don't understand. I thought we had talked about this already. Once it got towards the end, we would have you here, in our home, where you are comfortable."

She nodded, "I know we talked about that but I have changed my mind. I think I just want to be in the hospital or even a hospice facility, not here."

I didn't understand what had changed. Why would she want to be in a hospital environment instead of in her own bed? "Scotti, I thought we had this all figured out."

She slowly got up and, with my help, sat down on the coffee table right across from me. She placed her hands on the tops of my thighs and smiled, "Mason, I want you to hear me out on this, okay. Don't go all ape shit with me, just listen, please."

I definitely did not like the sound of this but against my better judgment, I agreed, "Okay."

"Mason, one of these days, there is going to be someone else in your life. You are going to find her, you are going to fall in love with her and you are going to marry her…"

"Scotti, NO!"

"Mason, please, you promised." She was so calm and cool and I felt like I was crawling out of my skin. I nodded, telling her to go on. "You are going to marry her and God willing you will have beautiful babies together. This home is just that, it is a home. It is the perfect home for a family and a perfect home to raise children in. If I take my last breath here, this home will be nothing but a terrible memory for you, and I can't do that. I can't do that to you, your future wife or your future children. It's not fair."

This home is mine and Scotti's, nobody else's and it never will be. I couldn't tell if I was hurt or pissed so I took a few deep breaths before I spoke. "Scotti, I appreciate what you are doing, I really do, but there will never, ever, be another woman in my life and certainly not children. You are my wife, you are the love of my life. There is no way you could ever be replaced."

"I am not asking you to replace me, Mason. I am asking you to not give up on love because I won't be here any longer. We both know what love can be like. Why would you not want to feel that again?"

I jumped up and started pacing, no longer having the ability to sit still and instead of talking, I yelled. "I have told you time and time again, you are it for me! YOU! Nobody else! I will respect your wishes to die in a hospice facility but it is not because I will someday have a wife and children living here. It is because that is what you want, and I will always give you what you want! That is the only reason!"

The tears were flowing down her face and I know I have upset her but I am sick of her thinking I could ever be with another woman after what we have shared together. I don't care how young I am. I don't care how healthy I am and how many years I have left to live. It will never happen. Instead of going over to my wife, comforting her and telling her I was sorry for yelling at her, I did the biggest asshole thing I could have done. I turned away from her, grabbed my keys and walked out the door.

Thirty Eight

Scotti

I knew this conversation wasn't going to be a pleasant one but I didn't think Mason would actually leave. I want to be mad and scream but I can't. Not only do I not have the energy, but I don't know how I would react if the tables were turned. I slowly got up off the table, took the two steps it takes to get to the couch and dropped myself down on it. I can't go chasing after Mason, beg him to talk to me or even apologize for trying to get him to move on without me. I can barely walk the couple of steps I just did so the only thing I can do is sit here and wait for him to get home.

I do believe Mason should not waste his life crying and angry over losing me. I do believe he needs to find a woman that he can fall in love with and I do believe that he would make an incredible father. If I am being honest though, the thought of him with someone else makes my insides feel like they are ripping apart, but there is no way I am going to tell him that. Those words would haunt him for the rest of his life and if he ever did find someone that he could potentially have a loving relationship with, my words would always be in the back on his mind and he would never fully give himself to that woman, so I am keeping my mouth shut.

After that talk and Mason leaving, I am feeling drained. Since there is no way I could possibly make it up to the bedroom by myself, I decide to just lay here on the couch and take a nap. My eyes are already extremely heavy but before I completely give in to the exhaustion, I think about the short time I have known Mason, the love that I feel for him and how incredibly lucky I am to be spending the end of my life with such an amazing man. I close my eyes and as I am falling deeper into sleep, I smile, knowing that even though he is mad now, we can work things out between us, because we have nothing but love for one another.

Mason

I knock lightly on the door, not knowing why I am here but not really knowing where else to go. "Mason, what are you doing here? Where is Scotti?" My aunt is standing in front of me and instead of answering her, I burst into tears and run into her arms, the same way I would when I was a child and I had a scraped knee.

We stand there in her doorway while I finish crying. She is hugging me and rubbing my back, telling me everything is going to be okay but she is wrong, everything is not going to be okay.

I start to calm down and pull away from her and wipe my face with the back of my hands, "I'm sorry, I don't know what got into me."

"Don't be sorry sweetie, I will always be here for you. But, please tell me, is Scotti alright?"

Aunt Rose and I have talked often and she has been over to our house for dinner twice. She has grown incredibly fond of Scotti so for me to burst in like this is probably scaring the hell out of her. "She is okay. Feeling pretty weak today which is why I should be home taking care of her but instead I ran away like a fucking piece of shit."

"Mason, what is going on?" She asked me.

I sighed then looked down, feeling like the worst husband on the planet, "She wanted to have a talk with me about what she wants to do at the very end of her life. Then she started talking to me about finding someone else and getting married again and I just lost it. I was so pissed that she could even think I would ever be with anyone else. I didn't know where to go so I came here."

Aunt Rose pointed over to the swing on the front porch so we both walked over there and sat down. She put her arm around me and pulled me close to her, "Sweetie, I can imagine that would be hard to hear but I think she is just trying to make sure you don't crawl into a hole and give up on living after she is gone. I am sure she didn't mean for it to make you mad."

"I understand that I guess, but, I don't want to even think about it. I know Scotti is not going to be with us much longer but she is still here now. Why is she so insistent on talking about the very end and after? We need to focus on now." A few tears fell down my cheek and I laid my head on Rose's shoulder, thanking God that I had her back in my life again.

"She is a planner, Mason. She is trying to make things as easy on you as possible. I wish Uncle Dale and I would have talked about what our wishes were after we passed. He died so unexpectedly and we never talked about it so I just didn't know. I wonder every single day if cremating him was what he would have wanted or if I failed him by doing that."

"Aunt Rose, you could never fail him. He loved you with all his heart. That much I do remember about the time I lived with you." And he really did. I never understood a love like that until I met Scotti.

"Scotti loves you too, Mason. She just wants what's best for you. Today, tomorrow and long after she is gone."

I knew Rose was right. We talked for a bit longer but I couldn't stand being away from Scotti anymore. I thanked her for everything, gave her a quick hug then ran to my truck so I could race home to my wife. I should have never left her. I should have sat with her and talked to her about how I was feeling instead of running away from her like I did. I had to get home to her and I hope like hell she would be able to forgive me.

Thirty Nine

Scotti

I was starting to come out of my fog. I don't know how long I had been sleeping but I was feeling a lot better than I was before I fell asleep. I slowly opened my eyes and when they focused, I saw Mason sitting next to me on the floor. He was rubbing my head and the look on his face almost broke me. I could tell he was feeling guilty about leaving, but honestly, I was just happy he was back at home. I reached out for his free hand and squeezed it and when I looked back in his eyes I could tell he had been crying.

"Honey, it's okay. I'm not mad." I really wasn't mad at all.

"You should be." Is all he said, and then looked down at our joined hands.

I just shook my head and squeezed his hand again. He laid his head on the couch next to mine and pulled my hand to his mouth and kissed it. I let go of his hand, then started rubbing his head and the second I started doing that he sat up and cried.

"I am so sorry, Scotti. I should have never taken off like that. I should have never left you, especially with you feeling so bad." He covered his face with his hands.

I slowly sat up then got off the couch so I was on my knees right next to him on the floor. Our knees were touching but he wouldn't look at me. I pulled his hands away then put my hands on each side of his face trying to force him to look at me. His eyes were closed and the tears were falling down so fast so I leaned in trying to kiss each one away to no avail. "Please Mason, open your eyes."

He slowly opened them then wiped his face. I dropped my hands from his face then grabbed each of his hands. He held his gaze on me so I gave him a smile. "I don't deserve your forgiveness, Scotti," he said.

"There is nothing to forgive, Mason." I told him sternly.

"You are sick and having a terrible day and I ran out of here angry, leaving you on your own," he shook his head, "you should be furious."

"I will admit, I was upset at first, but then I had to put myself in your shoes. I can't imagine how hard this is for you."

"That doesn't matter. You are who is most important."

"Mason, stop that! We are both getting fucked out of a life that we want more than anything. We are both losing something. We are both important in this, not just me." Right now though, I was thinking that what I was going through had to be a million times better than what he is going through.

"It's still not right, Scotti. I should have been an adult and talked to you, even if it was hard." The disappointment he had in himself was overwhelming and I couldn't bear to see him upset like this anymore. I pulled him against me and wrapped him into a tight hug. It took him a minute but he finally put his arms around me and pulled me closer.

We held each other tight and the only sound in the room was our breathing. He started to pull away from me and instead of looking at me, he gave me a quick kiss on the forehead then stood up and turned away from me. I stood up slowly, having to use the couch and coffee table to help me up. I groaned a little when I made it to my feet, causing him to turn around, "Fuck, baby, again! Again, I turned away from you and you needed my help!"

"Mason, it's fine, stop beating yourself up. If I needed help I would have just asked you." Although I really could have used the help, he was already feeling like shit so I wasn't going to add to that.

He shook his head then took a couple of deep breaths and opened his mouth like he was going to say something then quickly closed it.

"Honey, please, be open with me. Don't hold back anything." I didn't want him to ever feel like he was walking on egg shells around me. We were open with each other and I never wanted that to stop.

He took a deep breath then dropped to his knees, wrapped his arms around my waist and pulled me to him. He had his cheek lying on my stomach and I reached down and ran my fingers through his hair. "I'm scared, Scotti," he said quietly, "I am so scared I can't even think straight. When you got up this morning, and you were so weak, then you wanted to talk about what to do with your body after you die, I just lost it. I didn't know how to handle it. I knew it was something we would eventually have to talk about but I just wasn't prepared for it yet."

I hated that my disease was not only killing me, but it was breaking Mason. I never wanted this for him but in all honesty, I could have never gotten this far without him. I didn't know what to say. I didn't know what I could possibly do to comfort him so I continued rubbing his head.

He quickly stood up, put his hands on each side of my face and laid his forehead on mine to look me in the eyes, "I don't know how I am going to live without you," he was sobbing loudly, "I don't want to live a life without you in it."

I couldn't let him do this. I never wanted him to give up. I knew it would be hard to lose me, but I never wanted him to die right along with me. "Mason, please don't say that. Please, don't give up on yourself. You are young and healthy and have a lot of life to live."

He shook his head while crying, "No, No, No."

I didn't have the right words. I couldn't comfort him because I didn't know how. How could I possibly tell him that he would be okay? Would I be okay if the tables were turned? Would I be able to move on if Mason died? I can't imagine being able to love another person the way I loved Mason and I would have to love someone just as deeply to ever be able to move on with them.

I was torn.

Mason was in pain.

And suddenly I felt like a complete coward.

Forty

Mason

I lost it. I am supposed to be strong. I am supposed to be the one that holds it together. I am the man, isn't that what I am supposed to be doing? Well, I couldn't.

I rushed home, ready to get on my hands and knees and beg my wife for forgiveness but when I walked in and saw her sleeping on the sofa, everything changed. For the first time since we met I saw the cancer. For the first time since we met, I saw what this disease was really doing to her. She was pale and looked so tiny lying there. I left her standing in front of the sofa and that is as far as she made it before she had to lie down.

I fell to my knees next to her and stared. I didn't want to take my eyes off of her. I kept watching her, thinking that if I turned away, she would take her last breath. What scares me most about all of this is she is getting worse every day. She is weak and pale and simple things like getting up and down are difficult and will become even harder for her as the days and weeks go by.

How can I possibly let her go?

The answer is simple… I have no fucking choice in the matter. She was going whether I liked it or not.

Once I calmed a little from my breakdown, I gently picked her up, cradling her in my arms, then sat on the sofa, laying her in my lap and wrapping my arms around her as tight as her little body could handle.

"Mason, I am not going to break. You can hug me tighter than that." She knew me all too well. She knew I loved to hold her tight but if I was being honest, I did think she was going to break. I hugged her a little tighter, but not nearly how I wanted. She chuckled but didn't say anything and laid her head on my chest. We sat there in silence until the sun had set and it was starting to get dark.

"You have to be starving, baby. Can I get you something to eat?" I know she didn't have much of an appetite but I had not seen her eat all day so I needed to feed her.

"Sure, I could eat." She started to move from my lap.

"Where are you going?" I asked her.

"I thought we could get up and make some food together. I'd enjoy that," she quietly said.

I knew she was in no position to get up and cook anything but I also knew that telling her no would upset her, "I was actually thinking that maybe we could order a pizza, if that sounds good to you."

Her eyes lit up. Pizza is a favorite of Scotti's, so I knew that she would be okay with that.

"No answer is needed, I can see it in your face." I said smiling, making her giggle. I picked her up then set her on the cushion next to mine then reached in my pocket to grab my phone, "I will call and order it. Why don't you look and see if there are any good movies on TV that we can watch tonight."

She clapped her hands together, "My favorite! Pizza then snuggling up on the sofa together and watching movies."

Her smile was beautiful and perfect and even though I knew she felt horrible, something as little as ordering pizza and watching a movie made her face light up as bright as the sun. I knew with how tired she was that she would probably not make it through much of the movie but just being able to hold her and feel her next to me, awake or not, was all I needed. It was all I could possibly want because I knew, before too long, pizza and movies with her would be another distant memory.

After we ate, or in Scotti's case, nibbled, we laid on the couch to watch a movie. I knew she would fall asleep quickly but I don't even know if the opening credits were finished before I could hear the light snores next to me. I didn't want to let her go so I decided to finish the movie while holding her. Once it was over, I quietly got up to turn everything off then I picked up Scotti to take her to our bed.

When I got in the room I laid her down on her pillow, then went into the bathroom to clean up and get changed, careful not to wake her. Today was such an emotional day and between everything we talked about to running off to crying my eyes out, I felt dirty so I decided to take a quick shower. I got inside and the feeling of the warm water hitting my body felt incredible so this quick shower was turning into a long drawn out shower.

I put my hands against the cold tile and put my head down directly under the stream of water. My mind was racing and I was trying really hard to not think about how life was going to be when Scotti was gone, but I kept going back to that.

I continued to stand there, thinking about everything from my life growing up to the day I met Scotti, when I felt two small arms wrap around my waist from behind. I jumped then turned quickly to see my beautiful wife standing there, a smile on her face, wearing absolutely nothing.

"Baby, did I wake you?" I was trying to be quiet, knowing how much she needed her rest.

She shook her head, "No. I woke up and you were gone, then I heard the shower and decided to join you. I hope you don't mind." She bit her lip like she was a little embarrassed.

"Absolutely not, I never mind," I bent down to kiss her lips, "but how are you feeling? I don't want you to get too weak."

"I'm okay. I will admit I am not feeling as good as I was a week ago, but I am okay." I loved that she was honest with me and didn't try to sugarcoat how she was feeling. I also hated that she was honest with me, instead of sugarcoating how she was feeling.

"Let's get you back to bed. This water is starting to cool down and I don't want you getting cold." I turned off the faucet, opened the shower curtain and grabbed a towel for Scotti. She was already getting goosebumps on her body so I quickly wrapped it around her, picked her up and carried her to the bed. I was still dripping wet and hadn't even put a towel around me but I needed to warm her up so she didn't get sick.

The blankets were already pulled back from when she got out of bed so I laid her down and immediately pulled the blankets up to her neck and tucked them around her entire body. Her lips were chattering a little but all in all she was warming up pretty quickly.

I stood with her until the shivering stopped. She smiled at me then looked me up and down, reminding me that I still had not put a stitch of clothing on. I leaned in and kissed her then stood up to go get dressed. "Mason, wait." She said quickly.

I turned to look at her and she sat up, keeping the blankets tucked underneath her arms, "What is it, baby?"

"I don't want you to get dressed." She said smiling.

"So, you want me to stand here naked and get sick instead." I said, teasing her.

She laughed then reached for my hand, which I gladly gave to her. "No, of course not. I think there may be a way to warm you up without actually getting you dressed."

I knew where she was going with this and normally I would be all for it but she is sick, and weak. This couldn't work. "Scotti, baby, why don't we see how you are feeling tomorrow."

She shook her head, "Mason, I don't know if I will have a tomorrow."

"Please don't say that." That was the last thing I wanted to hear.

"I can feel it, Mason. I can feel things changing and tonight I feel well enough to make love to you. I just don't know that I will tomorrow."

I can't control the moisture that builds up in my eyes. I am so afraid of losing Scotti but I am also so afraid of making love to her and hurting her. How can I do this? She is weak and has been sleeping most of the day. Could I really say no to her? She smiled at me then dropped the blanket, showing me her perfect body and I had my answer. I could never say no to her, ever.

Forty One

Scotti

I could see in his face that he was torn. He was so afraid of hurting me, but I wasn't in any pain. Today had been a day of feeling weak and tired and with everything that happened with us, I couldn't think of a better way to end it than by making love to my husband.

Once I dropped the blanket from my body, I knew he was a sure thing. He climbed into bed next to me, covered us both up then started kissing me. In my whole life I have never been kissed like Mason kisses me and if all he ever wanted to do was kiss, I would be okay with that. I was pretty sure I could have an orgasm just from that alone.

He was being gentle, slowly caressing my arms and my body as he gently pushed his tongue inside of my mouth. I grabbed on to his shoulders and pulled him towards me and even though I knew I didn't have the strength to actually move him, his body immediately came my way. He straddled my body, not putting any kind of weight on me, and stared.

"Mason, what are you doing?" I asked him.

"Memorizing this moment. I want this burned into my brain so there is no chance I can ever forget it."

I smiled at him and let him look at every inch of me. Just when I thought he was going to start making love to me, he backed off again.

"Honey, it's okay, you won't hurt me," he wasn't budging so I put my hands on each side of his face, "Mason, I promise, it will be fine. Just please... go slow tonight."

He took a deep breath and a few tears fell out of his eyes, onto my chest. He slowly started lowering himself on to my body. I still had my hands on his face so I pulled him closer and started kissing him again. Our kisses were sweet and gentle and perfect. He reached down to position himself and slowly pushed himself inside of me, causing me to moan into his mouth.

"I love you so much." He whispered, as he started to gently move in and out of me.

"I love you, Mason." I said.

No other words were spoken while we made love. Our bodies were in sync and nothing in my life ever felt as good as this very moment. We couldn't keep our hands off each other and even though this was slow love making, it was the best sex we had ever had.

I didn't want to stop but I could feel myself on the brink of an orgasm and by the look on Mason's face and the way he was starting to tense up, I could tell he was too. It wasn't much longer and I was quietly having the most incredible orgasm of my life. He continued moving but within just a few more seconds, he was following me with his own orgasm.

He slowly laid his body on top of mine as we were both trying to catch our breath and come down from our high. Mason lifted his head, kissed my neck, cheek then mouth and slowly rolled off me and laid by my side. He pulled me up against him and I immediately buried my head in his neck. We held each other, both of us afraid of letting go. Mason lifted his head and looked into my eyes, "I will never forget this night, as long as I live."

I smiled at him and we stared at each other and in that moment, I think the realization of everything hit us, and the tears began for both of us. We knew there would never be any more nights like this. In all honestly, we probably shouldn't have done this tonight, but we both needed it. Mason needed this beautiful memory of the last time we made love to each other.

He laid his head on my chest while I lazily rubbed my finger up and down his back. I could feel his tears hitting my breasts and I am positive he could feel mine hitting the top of his head. We continued holding each other, refusing to close our eyes, scared of what tomorrow would bring. I wish I could freeze this night forever but instead, I silently prayed that Mason could hold on to this memory as a good one, not remember it as the night where he finally accepted that his wife would be leaving him forever.

Forty Two

Mason

Now

Scotti is not having a good day today. She has been tossing and turning, unable to get comfortable and refusing to eat or drink anything. I have done everything including get on my hands and knees and beg her to eat and drink and it is not working.

Currently, she is having a scan done to see what is going on in her body so I am sitting in her room, anxiously awaiting her return. Even though she is surrounded by several doctors and nurses, having her out of my sight is terrifying and I am so afraid something is going to happen to her while I am not around.

Aunt Rose has come by the hospital a couple of times to see her and I can tell that seeing her so sick like this has really been upsetting her. Scotti has a way of making people love her right away because of her beauty and smile and just her personality in general. I thought maybe I was insane for falling in love with her so quickly after we met but when I saw how fast that

Aunt Rose took a liking to her, I realized I would have been insane NOT to fall in love with her.

I look up and Scotti is being rolled back into the room and her eyes are closed. The nurse gets the bed adjusted and locked back into place, reconnects her I.V. then adjusts her blanket. I have moved to her side and am holding her hand that feels like a block of ice.

"Mr. Shaw?" I look over at the nurse, "Dr. Hammond will be coming in soon to discuss some things with the two of you, but we are going to wait a little bit so Mrs. Shaw can get a little more rest."

I just nod at her then lift the blanket to place Scotti's freezing hand underneath. As much as I want to keep a hold of it, I need her to warm up. I lay my head next to her small body and doze off a little until I hear the doctor walk in.

"Good evening, Mason. How is our favorite patient doing?" At the sound of his voice, Scotti slowly turns her head so she is looking at the doctor and smiles. "I always love to see that smile." He says, smiling back at her.

I have always liked Dr. Hammond. He takes incredible care of my wife and treats her like she is his own family. I reach under the blanket, take

Scotti's hand again and bring it to my mouth then gently place it back under the blanket. She smiles at me then we both turn to look at the doctor.

"Well, as you know, we did her scan to see where the cancer is at right now," Doctor Hammond is looking at both of us, "unfortunately what we saw, was not good."

My heart dropped.

Dr. Hammond looked at Scotti and even though he is a doctor and deals with this every day, I think I could see a bit of moisture building up in his eyes. "Scotti, right now, you are bleeding internally. Everything is starting to shut down and the pain level is going to get quite intense and it's going to happen very quickly." I wanted to be strong but I could feel the tears falling, "I think it's time we start you on the medicine you need to make you comfortable and help you to feel pain free."

This was it. As soon as they injected that medicine into her, I would never be able to talk to her again, never be able to look into her eyes again. I knew this was coming, but I was not at all prepared for it. Scotti looked over at me and I looked at her and she gave me a weak smile. I leaned in and kissed her forehead and when I did she placed her hand on my cheek and whispered, "I'm ready to go, Mason."

I pulled away to look at her and instead of seeing tears, her face looked peaceful. I nodded, not able to say anything and not wanting to turn away from her. She turned to look at the doctor and repeated to him what she said to me, "I'm ready."

I turned to look at the doctor and he nodded his head then looked over at the nurse who immediately walked out of the room. "The nurse is going to get the medicine all ready and we will inject the first dose into you in about fifteen minutes," he looked over to me sadly, "Mason, I know this is not what any of us wanted but we all knew it would get to this." He reached over to shake my hand then walked to the other side of Scotti's bed and gave her a hug, "Your strength is incredible Scotti but now it's time for the medicine to take over, so you will no longer be suffering."

She smiled at him, "Thank you Dr. Hammond," her voice was incredibly weak but she was able to get a couple of words out at a time.

He rubbed the top of her head, shook my hand again then made his way out of the room. I had only minutes to tell my wife every single thing I wanted to tell her and yet, I couldn't get one word to come out of my mouth. She pulled her hand out of under the blanket, put it on top of mine and lightly squeezed it. "I love you, Mason, forever."

Forty Three

Scotti

"I love you, Mason, forever." As soon as those words were out of my mouth, he broke down. I didn't know how to comfort him. In just a matter of minutes, we would never have another conversation again. The doctor had just told me that I was pretty much done for and for the first time since I found out I had cancer, I was at peace with dying. I have been stalling on taking any kind of medication that would put me to sleep because I couldn't stand not seeing Mason's face anymore, so I dealt with the pain and put up with the discomfort.

When the doctor told me it was time that I take that medicine, for the first time I was finally ready to let go. I was finally ready to leave this Earth and go on to whatever my next journey is. I was finally going to be cancer free. I couldn't take Mason with me, but I had the best memories to carry with me. I knew, one day, Mason and I would be together again and that in itself gave me incredible peace.

Mason's nightmare is just beginning but I hope that when he leaves here, without me by his side, that he really thinks about everything we talked about and he really lives his life, a life that he deserves. He will always have me in his heart, he will always remember our time together and I will always be his first love and that is okay. All I want is for him to get out there and live. I want him to live a life that makes him happy. If that means never marrying and having children, then so be it, as long as he is happy.

We hear a sound and both look up right as the nurse is walking in to my room with a syringe filled with medicine. This is it. This is when I have to say goodbye to my husband. I don't know how long I will live after this medicine enters my body, but I do know that this will be the last time I ever have my eyes open again. I stare; really stare, into Mason's red and puffy eyes, wishing like hell I could take his pain away. The nurse starts to walk over to my I.V but Mason quickly turns to her, "WAIT!" He yells, making the nurse jump. "I'm sorry, but can you give us just five more minutes, please."

She gives him a sad smile, nods her head then walks out of the room. Mason takes a deep breath and lets it out slowly, "I have things to say first," he says, then grabs both of my hands.

Forty Four

Mason

I couldn't just let the nurse inject that shit until I had one last talk with my wife. I have told her a million times how I feel about her but I felt like I needed to tell her again, one last time. I needed those words to be the last words she hears before she closes her eyes.

I pull both of her hands to my mouth and kiss them. "I know I have said it at least a million times but I have to say it again one last time. Scotti, stumbling across you on that beach was the best thing that has ever happened to me. The second I saw you, I literally fell over because of your beauty and as soon as you spoke to me, I knew you were someone that was going to change my life forever. When you walked away that day at the beach my heart felt like it was breaking and I knew I needed to find you.

I felt like I was in a race to say everything I needed to say. Of course, this race had no winner. "Once I found you, I knew I would never let you go again and when you told me you were sick and you didn't have long to live, I never once thought about walking away. My heart beats every day because of you. There will never be a day that goes by that I won't be thinking about you and I would be fucking lying right now if I was to tell you that this doesn't hurt because this hurts like hell. I feel like there is a knife stabbing away at my heart. I know I should be sitting here, telling you that everything is going to be okay but I refuse to lie to you, especially now."

Scotti reaches up and wipes the tears that are falling down my face, "Mason…"

"Wait, let me finish this because I am down to about three minutes before that nurse comes back in," she nods her head. "Even though the pain that I feel right now is horrible, I will never, for a second, regret the time I had with you. You have made everything dark turn to light. I never thought light even existed in my world until I met you. There is not a damn thing that I don't love about you and for all the rest of my days, you will be the reason that I have that light."

I know I am just rambling but I am trying to get everything out before I am out of time, "I love you more than I have ever loved anyone before in my entire life and I will continue to love you more than anyone. I promise you, I will make an effort to live after you are gone, and I promise you I will try because all I want to do is make you proud of me. I never want you to be watching me and feel any kind of disappointment so for you, I promise to live." Just saying that hurts like hell but when I make a promise to my wife, I keep it.

"I have studied you for months. Touched every single inch of your body and stared into your eyes so that there is nothing that I will be forgetting when you are no longer here. You will never be gone from me in here," I point at my heart, "because you have permanently implanted yourself directly in there and there is no way you will ever leave me."

Scotti's is crying but she is also smiling so I feel good about making her feel loved because I certainly didn't want our last conversation to make her upset. I crawl up next to her on the bed, put my lips on hers and gently kiss her, letting them linger there and not wanting to pull away. I hear someone clear their throat and look up to see the nurse standing there. Scotti looks over at her and nods silently telling her to go ahead with the drug then looks back over at me.

"Mason, thank you for allowing me to live what was left of my life with a smile on my face and love in my heart," she takes a couple of breaths then continues, "you are my angel, my knight in shining armor and the love of my life," a couple more breaths, "I am so incredibly in love with you and I don't think I would have lived nearly as long as I did if I would have never met you."

She has to take another break but I know she doesn't have long because the nurse has already walked out of the room. "I love you so much, Mason." Her words are getting slower and her eyes are getting heavier, "Mason…"

I lean into her and whisper in her ear, "Sleep, baby. I love you for all eternity."

"I love you," She whispers then closes her eyes completely and when her breath evens out I know that I just heard the last words I would ever hear from her. I laid my head down next to hers, listened to her light breathing and held her close. I kiss her cheek and pull the blanket up over the both of us. My entire life has just shattered.

Forty Five

Mason

It has been over twenty four hours since Scotti has been given the sedative and I have refused to leave her side. Aunt Rose brought me some food but even walking into the bathroom has scared me. I don't want her to be alone when she takes her last breath. I am sitting in a chair, next to Scotti's bed, holding her hand when I hear a strange sound coming out of her. I look at her face and she almost looks pained, and her breathing is very shallow. I hit the call button about ten times and a nurse is inside almost immediately.

"What is going on?" I ask, pointing at Scotti, with a raised voice.

The nurse takes a look at her then puts a stethoscope to her chest. When she pulls it away she gives me a pained look, "Mr. Shaw, it won't be too long. Her body is shutting down."

Of course I knew this was happening but I didn't like what I was seeing, "Dr. Hammond told us this would be peaceful but she does not look peaceful!"

"I promise you, it is peaceful for her. It's just part of the…"

I cut her off, "Process! Fuck, I have heard that a million times!" I take a deep breath, "Sorry. I just want to make sure she is not feeling any pain at all."

"I will give her a little more sedative and see if that helps."

"Thank you." I sit back down on my chair and the nurse leaves to get the medicine and is back in within a couple minutes. She injects it into the I.V., waits a minute until Scotti calms down then leaves the room.

I have been reading a lot about the end of life and whether or not people can hear you and a lot of things I have read says that they can. Scotti seems like she is holding on and as much as it pains me to say it, I need to let her go. I lean into her and whisper in her ear, "You can go, Scotti. I will be okay. The love that you gave me will assure me that I will be okay. I love you so much and I will never, ever stop loving you."

I sit back on my chair, holding her hand and stare as her breaths are getting further and further apart. Just when I think she has taken her last breath, another one comes along. I watch this process for a long time until she takes one long breath in… and nothing comes out. I watch her, waiting, looking at her chest for any sign of life, watching to see if any part of her body moves, but nothing is happening.

I buzz the nurse and when she walks in and sees the look on my face she doesn't say a word. She puts her stethoscope in her ears, holds it to Scotti's chest, and listens. She then stands, removes the stethoscope and wraps it around her neck, "She's gone."

Those are the two words I have been dreading since the day I heard about Scotti's cancer. I knew they were coming, I mean, I whispered in her ear and told her to let go, but that doesn't make hearing the words any easier. I lay my head on her chest and I cry. I wrap my hands around her frail and cold body and I squeeze her as hard as I can.

All I hear is screaming, it is so loud that it is making my ears hurt and when I lift my head and look around, I realize there is nobody else in the room and the screaming is coming from me. I look back at her beautiful face, hoping the nurse was wrong, but nothing is there. Scotti is dead.

I rub my hands down her arm, I pet her hair and I kiss her forehead, her cheek and her neck. I pull the blankets up around her because she is so cold and she hates being cold. I pull her hand to my lips and just hold it there.

As time goes on her body is looking paler. I don't want to leave her here, I want her to open her eyes, be cured and we can go to the beach and watch the sunset. I lay my head back down then I feel hands on each of my shoulders. When I look up, Aunt Rose is standing there. I gently lay Scotti's hand down, then stand up and practically fall into Rose's arms. I am sobbing so loud and only getting louder and Rose is just holding me and letting me cry.

After several minutes I pull away from her and go back to sit on my chair next to Scotti. "Mason, sweetie, there are some papers that you need to fill out and take care of."

"What kind of papers?" I never take my eyes off Scotti's face.

"The hospital needs to know which funeral home will be picking Scotti up."

I shake my head, "No! I can't let her go. They can't take her!"

"Sweetie, she is gone. I'm so sorry. I wish I could take this pain away from you." Rose is now crying and all I am thinking about is the fact that she wants me to leave. She wants me to leave Scotti lying in this bed, alone. The thought of leaving her makes me sick, but I know it has to be done.

“Can you give me a couple of minutes with her, alone?” I ask Aunt Rose.

“Of course, sweetie. I will be right outside in the hall.” She kisses my cheek then walks out of the room.

I kiss Scotti’s hand again and it seems like every time I do, it feels colder. “I don’t know if you can hear me right now or if you are looking over me right now but if you are and you can hear this, I just want to tell you once again that I love you so much, baby. I promise you, there is nobody walking the face of this Earth that was loved as much as you were. I hope you are at peace and please know that I will never, ever let you leave my heart.” I kiss her hand and her lips then stand up and pull the blankets up to her chest. I make my way to the door then turn around to look at my wife one last time, “I love you, Scotti, forever,” I tell her, then walk away from the only woman I have ever loved.

Epilogue

Scotti has been gone for six months and there is not a second that goes by that I don't think about her. I can still smell her in our home, on our sheets and pillowcases, everywhere. Everything that she placed in the house is still in the exact spot she left it. I can't bring myself to change anything and to be honest, I don't know if I ever will be able to.

A couple weeks after she died, I knew I needed to get out of bed and out of the house so I threw myself into my business, focusing on only that, like I did before Scotti and I met. When I would get home at night, I would sit on the couch and stare at the urn that her ashes lie in and cry. This stainless steel urn that has an engraving of a beautiful angel on it is now holding my wife. I had more tears than I ever knew was humanly possible and just when I thought I couldn't cry more, I did.

Most mornings I would have to force myself to get out of bed to get to work because my nights had been restless with nightmares about watching Scotti die. After about a month, the nightmares turned into beautiful dreams. Instead of seeing her take her last breath, I saw her walking on the sand, laughing at me at the amusement park, kissing my lips, telling me she loved me. I was finally excited about going to sleep because I knew, that was when I would be with Scotti again.

It is almost sunset and I am sitting at our beach, next to the urn that holds my wife. This is the exact spot that we met and it brings me great comfort to come here. So much so that I am here at least five times a week but tonight is different. Tonight is the night that I am finally going to scatter her ashes in the ocean, just as she asked me to do. It took a long time to get to this point and honestly I wasn't planning on ever scattering them… until I found the video.

One day, I was going through my phone and came across a video on there that I didn't remember taking. I pushed play on it and when I did I almost fell off the chair I was sitting on. Scotti filled up the screen with a huge smile on her face, talking to me and very much alive. She had done this the day I left it behind when I had to go to work and never said a word about it. The first time I realized what it was, I immediately stopped it, not sure if I could listen to her voice but after just a few minutes, I knew I couldn't live without hearing her again, so I pushed play.

"Hi, Mason.

I don't know how long it will take you to find this but when you do I hope you listen to what I have to say. First, I love you. I can never

say that enough but I will say it again, I love you. You have taught me that true love actually exists in this world when I never ever thought it was possible. You have made my life a life worth living. I know that living in this world without me is going to be hard, but you have to keep the memories that we made alive. Just think what life would have been like if we had never met. I am so glad that I went to the beach that day and I am so glad that you decided to go to the beach that day and even though I would have loved to have years with you, not just months, my time with you was the most incredible time I have ever had and I wouldn't change it for the world.

There will probably be nights that you are angry and want to hit something and you know what I want you to do? I want you to hit something. Just don't hit anything too hard so you don't break your hand.

You are allowed to feel angry and you are allowed to feel sad. I just don't want that anger and sadness to take over your life. You have a successful business so maybe start with focusing on that. Then, when you are ready, maybe go out with one of the guys from work and shoot some pool or something. Get yourself out there Mason. Don't lock yourself away until you die. This world is huge and you deserve to see it. You deserve every good thing that ever comes your way and you know why? You found a dying woman, and instead of pushing her away, you pulled her in, you loved her unconditionally and you made her feel happy. You made what was supposed to be a horrible time, not so horrible. You are special, Mason because there aren't too many people out there that would do something like that.

I want you to live, honey. I want you to experience things that you and I never got to experience together. I will always be in your heart just like you are always going to be in mine. You still have our beach and once my ashes are in those waters, it will be ours forever, and nothing can ever take that away from us.

Before I turn this off I want to say thank you, Mason. Thank you for loving me and thank you for allowing me to love you back. There are so many people out there who never get to experience love and I am thankful to say I am not one of those people. Our love story was the best of the best. Did we have the typical 'Happily Ever After?' No. But, what we did have was more than anyone could ever ask for and because of that, our love will never die. I love you, Mason, forever. Remember me always."

I had to finally turn off my phone because I had watched that video at least a hundred times. I have pictures of Scotti but I never thought I would hear her voice again. It was a gift that I never knew I needed. The first few times I watched it I couldn't stop crying but after that it started to bring me comfort. Once I really listened to everything that she said on that video, I knew it was time that I respected her wishes, and scattered her ashes.

The sun is right above the waters and this is the time that Scotti was the happiest. I unscrewed the cap from the urn and put it on the sand next to me then stand up and walk over to the water. I say a prayer that Scotti is finally at peace and I tell her I love her again before I tip the urn over. Her ashes slowly start falling and just as they are hitting the water, the waves are swallowing them up. I keep pouring until there is nothing left, then set the urn down next to me and stand there watching as the sun continues to set.

I look over and I can see her perfectly right now. She is sitting with her feet buried in the sand and her chin resting on her bent knees. Her smile is wide and getting even wider as she looks at the sun and I know she is feeling peaceful and content. After the sun has set, she stands up, grabs her shoes and practically skips away. Sunsets brought her joy when she had nothing else and sunsets brought us together.

I pick up the urn and the lid then start walking off the beach.

I turn back to look at the water and only the very top of the sun is still left to go down. I watch until there is nothing left and I smile, "I love you, baby, forever." I still have anger inside of me because Scotti was taken away and I still cry for her every single day but I do feel a sense of peace knowing that she is no longer suffering, because at the end, she really did.

I turn to leave, and as lonely as I am without her, I know I will see her again someday. That is what gets me through the long days without her. Scotti once said that the sunset that happens right after a storm was always the most beautiful. Scotti's cancer was the storm and now she is the beautiful sunset that I get to see every day and will continue to see until her and I are together again, for all eternity.

The End

Thank you...

Pat- You have endured hundreds of hours of being ignored by me, watching me go through the many emotions of writing this book and dealing with my looks of evil when you interrupt me. For all of that I say THANK YOU! Thank you for being my #1 supporter throughout all of this. Thank you for believing in me! I love you forever!!

Grandma- For loving me and supporting me no matter what... even when I told you about some of the content I was writing. You are an amazing woman with more strength than I could ever have. I love you!

To my boys- Even though you have both given me lots of gray hair over the years...You are both amazing young men and you make me very proud each and every day!! I love you both!

Colleen Noyes/Itsy Bitsy Book Bits- I don't even know where to begin. From our very first email you have been nothing but completely supportive and helpful, answering every question (and I have had A TON OF THEM!), making amazing teasers and ultimately becoming a great friend. Thank you for everything you have done and continue to do to make this experience even more amazing! There seriously aren't enough THANK YOU'S in the world for you ☺ Love you! XOXO

To my incredibly wacky and crazy co-workers- I couldn't possibly write a book without acknowledging all of you at the end! You are all an amazing group of people and I can't imagine my life without you! Thanks for the laughter more than anything. I definitely needed that, especially while writing this book!

Terror Twin- what would I be able to do if I didn't have you as my next door office neighbor? Also, who would steal my food if you didn't bring Nacho to work? Thanks for being such a great friend ☺ I love you!

Elizabeth- my blurb writer extraordinaire! I love you and can't think you enough for the help you give me! You saved my butt! LOL

Jayna and Lisa- thank you for all of your help once again! I not only love the feedback you each give me but your support means so much to me! Love you both!

To my family, friends and everyone out there who has given my novels a chance… THANK YOU! THANK YOU!! THANK YOU!!

XOXOXOXO

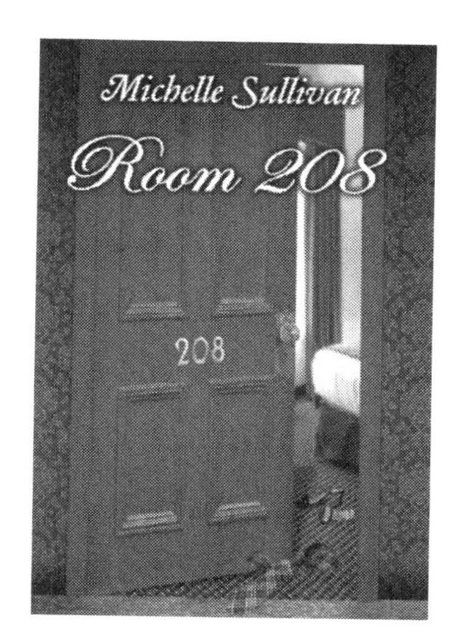

Look for these other great

novels by Michelle Sullivan

Available on:

Made in the USA
Middletown, DE
22 February 2019